OTHER GREAT TI

DISCIP
DISCIPLI
(Also available tit

CW00428915

BEYOND DO

Contact
Lisasimons65@gmail.com

The Humiliation of Sharon
CHAPTER TWO
Off to the shops.

'Here's your basket,' said Caroline. 'We only need a few things from here.'

Sharon followed Caroline as she made her way to the vegetable section, one hand tugging on the short skirt Caroline had made her wear, together with the white socks, buckled shoes and white blouse. She looked ridiculous, dressed far too young for her age, and her hair in bunches! That had nearly sent her into a fit, only the threat of a hairbrush spanking made her swallow her words and saw her now, in the supermarket, dressed like a teen or younger, meekly following her sister-in-law.

As Caroline examined several hands of ginger before selecting the largest, Sharon's memory tickled her thoughts, but she couldn't quite grasp the significance of that spice. The huge courgette however, together with an assortment of large carrots and a cucumber left nothing to her imagination and her tummy fluttered with nerves as she followed Caroline through the aisles to the chemist section where condoms and lubricant joined her collection of phallic vegetables.

'Ummmm, let's see,' said Caroline, scanning the checkouts.

'We could use the self service,' said Sharon. 'They're empty.'

Caroline laughed.

'Silly girl, where's the fun in that. No, I'm just deciding whether you should queue at the young lady's till or the young gentleman's.'

Sharon knew her face was red and Caroline needed to give her a firm push to get her feet moving towards the young man's checkout.

As she waited in line, Caroline slipped away and made her way around to the other side, so she could watch without being associated with the purchases.

'Next, please.'

Sharon placed her basket on the desk and slowly handed the checkout clerk each item.

'Nice day,' he said.

'Yes, lovely.'

'Planning something special?'

'Special?'

'To cook. Vegetarian I'm guessing?'

The clerk visible reddened as he took the condoms from her, his eyes darting to the collection of phallic vegetables piled up waiting to be bagged.

'Yes,' said Sharon, 'a vegetable hotpot.'

The clerk nodded as he scanned the large tube of lubricant.

When nothing happened, no expected beep as it registered, he tried again.

'Odd,' he said, more to himself, trying to scan the lube again. 'Oh, I see, the bar code has been scratched off. I'll just be one moment.'

Sharon expected to burst into flames at any moment; such was the humiliation coursing through her. Customers behind were looking over her shoulder at her items, she was sure of it, and then she jumped as the check-out boy's voice filled the air.

'Price check, check-out four. Price check, please.'

Turning his attention back to Sharon.

'It will just be a moment; perhaps we can bag these other items up?'

Sharon looked at Caroline who shook her head.

'Not just yet,' said Sharon. 'It's an all-or-nothing purchase I'm afraid.'

'That's quite all right, Miss, your purchase will complete, we just need a price.'

'All the same, I'll wait.'

'As you wish, Miss.'

'What's up, Mark?'

'Price check, please, Lisa' said Mark, handing the lubricant to a young woman.

'Right you are,' said Lisa with a smile.

Sharon blushed as she watched Lisa's face colour slightly as she looked at the item before she went off.

Upon her return, Sharon watched Lisa's eyes scan her purchases, and she just died as Lisa winked at her.

'That's the extra large one,' said Lisa. 'Eight Ninety-nine.'

'Thank you, Lisa,' said Mark, keying in the price and adding the lubricant to the pile.

Sharon handed her card over and quickly stashed the items into her bag.

'Just enter your pin, Miss.'

Sharon did so, her tummy fluttering as the thought of Caroline blocking her card or damaging the magnetic strip teased her mind, but no, the card and pin was accepted and she was through the checkout.

'Took your time,' said Caroline brightly. 'Next shop.'

*

When Sharon saw the sign, she felt oddly more relaxed than when paying for her purchases in the supermarket. After all, anyone *inside* a sex shop was there for the same purpose as Caroline and herself, to buy sex toys. At least, that's the assumption she made as they entered the shop.

Eyes widening, Sharon was amazed at the size of the shop, the variety of items, clothing and gadgets, and the array of colourful boxes stacking the shelves, but what caught and drew her further in were the staggering assortment of dildos and vibrators on offer. From every shape to every size, including some eye watering lengths and girths, and some, quite simply, impossible to comprehend, sizes.

'Can I help you?'

Sharon turned to see the shop assistant approaching Caroline.

'Yes please, can you point me to your Dominance, Bondage, and Sadomasochism section please?'

Sharon's cheeks warmed as the assistant glanced her way and smiled.

'Certainly, Mistress. If you would like to come this way.'

Sharon followed Caroline through the aisles and on through a beaded curtain, to a wonderland of whips, crops, canes, paddles, hairbrushes, and more, all dotted around manikins dressed in various leather outfits, mostly dominant but some clearly submissive, with their hoods, eyes and mouth zipped, breast and lower openings also zipped. Others were nothing more than a serious of straps that criss crossed the body. Sharon's fingers reached out to touch two integral dildos within a pair of panties and shivered, as they were long, thick, and studded with nodules.

'You like?'

Sharon gave a start then shook her head, snatching her fingers away.

'We'll take one,' said Caroline.

'Yes, Mistress,' said the shop assistant. 'Small, medium, or large.'

Caroline gave Sharon an appraising look.

'Extra large.'

'Yes, Mistress.'

Sharon let out a soft gasp. Not in dismay, shock or despair, but in response to her pussy clenching almost painfully tight in response to the purchase. Sharon blushed as she caught Caroline's raised eyebrow and was relieved when she turned away, breaking eye contact, allowing her to breathe once more.

'The canes,' asked Caroline. 'I presume the thicker ones hurt more, leave more of a welt?'

'Actually, it's all dependent on the wielder and the recipient,' said the assistant. 'These thin ones can impart quite the sting, whereas these thicker ones are more thuddy, the pain sinks deeper into the tissue of the bottom.'

'Show me,' said Caroline.

'Mistress?'

'Sharon,' said Caroline, 'out of those clothes and bend over.'

Having been made to strip down and redress in the car park, now wearing nothing more than a long jumper to cover her nudity, it took only seconds for Sharon to obey, something she realised she had done without hesitation when the cane tapped its length across her bottom.

The hiss of the bamboo as it cut through the air gave her a second's warning before its bite blazed across her cheeks.

She leapt up, grabbing her bottom with both hands, rubbing furiously.

Caroline chuckled.

'I see what you mean. Now the thick one.'

Sharon watched mutely as the assistant pulled out a long thick cane from the rack.

'If you would bend over, Miss.'

Sharon turned, bending and offering her bottom, ripples of fear, laced with curiosity and surprisingly, arousal, all fizzed through her body.

The jingle of the shop's door alerted them to another customer.

Sharon started to rise when she felt a hand on her back and heard Caroline say, 'Of course, go see if they need anything.' Caroline added, 'Stay where you are, Sharon, legs a little further apart.'

Shuffling her feet a little wider, Sharon bent further forwards, offering her bottom and pussy to the full view of Caroline and anyone else who might happen to step through the curtain.

A few minutes passed before the shop assistant returned.

'Sorry about that, Mistress, the gentleman is just browsing.'

'That's perfectly ok,' said Caroline. 'Perhaps I can help. You work on commission, right?'

'Yes, Mistress, mostly at least, I do get a small wage.'

Caroline nodded and Sharon heard the beads rattle behind her.

'Sir, if I may. I have my servant girl through there, if you spend $200, I'll have her suck you off, spend over $250, and you can fuck her. Interested?'

'Is she a looker?'

'Not really, but any hole's a goal, am I right?'

Sharon's face burned with humiliation and indignation, but she remained in place, conscious

12

the assistant would no doubt tattle whilst, no doubt, having a good look at her private parts to boot.

'Good. I'll leave you to browse.'

The crackle of the beads heralded Caroline's return and the tap, tap, tap of the cane brought Sharon back to her immediate fate. The snap sounded loud in her ears, the thud of the cane as it struck her bottom sent the pain flaring across her cheeks and, as advised, slowly sunk into the tissues of her bottom.

Cool fingers touched her cheeks, sharp nails digging into the two welts the strokes had left behind.

'I've made my choices,' came a man's voice, followed by the sound of the beads. '$280 by my reckoning.'

Caroline's hand prevented Sharon from rising once again.

'Good man, the assistant will ring them up and pack your items whilst you enjoy my servant here.'

Sharon's mind was whirling around as she remained, bent at the waist, hands on her knees, legs apart, waiting for some unknown, unseen man to fuck her.

'No need, she's on the pill,' she heard Caroline's voice.

Sharon's mind was so awash with emotions it was hard to pull out any specific one. Horrified, scared, and shame warred with arousal, trepidation, anticipation and desire. She gasped as she was entered, the thrust taking her by surprise, the force causing her to take a step forwards, the man's firm grip on her hips preventing her from toppling over. As she was fucked, her body burned from the heat of humiliation as her mind lashed her with images of what she must look like. The man himself only added to her shame, exclaiming how wet she was, though the wet slurping slapping noises already provided an adequate soundtrack to evidence that. Her breath too was faster, more gasping, her sighs became moans, cries pure sex as her arousal mounted, and this only further horrified her.

The sting of her hair pulling against her scalp focused her mind as her head was pulled up and she found herself staring at the back of Caroline's camera, the realisation she was being filmed, more expected than shocking still ramped up her cocktail of emotions; humiliation and desire racing neck and neck for the lead.

What was unexpected, and equally shocking to Sharon was her orgasm, which struck hard and fast as her pussy filled with hot wet cum from a total stranger.

She cried out, her hips bucking, pushing herself backwards, taking in as much cock as she could as her orgasm wracked her body with waves of incredible ecstasy.

Another moan escaped as her pussy clench tight around the cock as it pulled out, leaving her empty and needy. A slap across her bottom brought her out of her post fuck fog.

'Behave, slut, anyone would think you wanted more.'

Sharon dropped her head lower, pushing her bottom out earning her another slap.

'Oh, you shameless whore,' said Caroline.

Sharon heard the feminine and masculine laughter behind her and burned with shame, whilst her pussy clenched.

'Ohhh, she's dripped. Let me get a cloth.'

'No, get a dish, if you have one, or a glass.'

'Yes, Mistress.'

Sharon heard the words and knew the fate that awaited her. Not satisfied she had taken a strangers cum into her pussy, she would now be expected to drink it, swallow it and she shivered as a small orgasm rippled through her.

The Humiliation of Sharon
CHAPTER FOUR
The Surrogate Mistresses.

Sharon had barely crawled halfway up the hallway before she was ordered to halt, though it didn't come as a surprise. As she moved, she could hear Laura's friends remarking on her anus and it being bleached. Something Caroline had taken her for just a few days after her punishment begun and had already had two sessions. Both times, she had suffered an uncomfortable stinging sensation though the one time she had complained about it she had been soundly spanked, the humiliation tripled as the Doctor and nurse were both present at the time. Only the knowledge the Family used only the very best and the very discrete comforted her that her semi-public spanking would remain in the strictest of confidences.

'Reach back and spread your cheeks,' ordered Laura.

Obeying, Sharon cringed as her opening was so lewdly displayed and discussed.

'Did it hurt?'

'Not at first,' said Sharon.

'You will refer to Amy as Mistress Amy, and Lisa as Mistress Lisa, is that understood.'

'Yes, Mistress Laura.'

'Good girl,' said Laura.

'You said not at first,' prompted Amy.

'Yes, Mistress Amy, during the application it was ok but shortly after it stung, a lot.'

'I'd do that,' said Lisa.

'Not sure I would,' said Laura. 'Having my pussy waxed was painful enough.'

'Ohhhh, I just shave it. Much easier.'

'Me too,' said Amy.

'I can't be bothered shaving my bits every day,' said Laura. 'Waxing may sting, but it lasts a whole lot longer. Come on or we'll not have enough time to really enjoy ourselves. Move, Auntie.'

Sharon resumed her humiliating crawl into the main living space of her apartment.

'Go into the corner then place your head to the floor, bottom up nice and high. Girls, let's explore.'

Sharon's tummy flipped at the girls' excited laughter as they dashed off to her bedroom. Being a

18

small apartment, she could hear their chatter easily so could follow their discoveries.

'Doesn't your Aunt live with your Uncle Grant?' asked Lisa.

'Of course,' said Laura. 'But Mom sends her here when she wants to visit and punish her. Something about creating submissive memories amongst all her old possessions as well as her new ones at Uncle Grant's home and the Family home. Not sure I understand it all, but here, we should find stuff she wouldn't want Grant to see, like this!'

Sharon could only guess what Laura had found, though it became clear pretty quickly.

'Oh my gawd, look at that thing, it has two bits.'

'One goes up the bottom,' said Laura.

'Which one?' asked Lisa. 'They both look so big.'

'I think, that one,' said Amy, 'see they both curve, so my guess, they curve upwards.'

'What do we have here?' asked Lisa.

'Seems like your Auntie enjoys being tied down,' said Amy.

'Leave them on the bed, we can tie her down a little later and have a little play.'

'You are mean,' said Amy.

'Aunt Sharon stopped Uncle Grant from buying me a car. She's going to pay for that.'

'You think we'll get into trouble?' asked Lisa.

'No. Mom said we were to put some effort and imagination into it, otherwise she will spank each of us.'

'What!' said Amy. 'There's no way I'm getting a spanking from your Mom.'

'Me neither. I couldn't sit comfortably for days after my last one.'

'Then make sure to spank my Aunt good,' said Laura. 'Mom will check.'

'I'm going to use this,' said Amy, the sound of a meaty thwack followed. Sharon knew they had found the hairbrush Caroline had made her buy.

'I'll use the paddle,' said Lisa.

'That leaves the strap for me,' said Laura.

'Come on, let's head back, and get started,' said Laura. 'We'll start with hand spankings.'

More giggles and palatable excitement announced the girls return and within moments, Sharon found herself over the knee of Laura, who had pulled her skirt up to reveal her slender, tanned thighs for Sharon to place herself over.

The spanking was hard and fast and despite only being just twenty, hours of tennis practice gave her a strong right arm that soon had Sharon's feet kicking.

'Oh my gawd,' said Lisa.

'What?' asked Laura, her hand still rising and falling.

'I never realised just how much you can see,' said Lisa, her hands over her red face.

'Really?' asked Amy.

Lisa shook her head.

'And I've been spanked in front of my brother sooooo many times.'

Amy and Laura laughed, Laura's hand barely faltering as she continued to spank Sharon.

'To be fair, I doubt you are as sexually aroused as Sharon is,' said Amy.

'Sexually aroused?' asked Lisa.

'Seriously?' said Amy. 'Look.'

Now, many spankees will tell you that it is very embarrassing being spanked in front of others but once that hand starts to land, all thought, other than the pain in one's bottom, vanishes. Not so for Sharon. Whilst a good part of her thoughts were focused solely on the pain radiating within her bottom, there was still a part that was following the conversation and her embarrassment was slowly turning to mortification.

'See how thick and puffy her lips are?' asked Amy. 'That's 'cause she is sexually aroused. And see, her vagina is actually gaping, that's not normal, unless turned on.'

'I see, so mine doesn't look like that then, when I am spanked,' said Lisa. 'That's a relief, I mean, you can see her clit and everything.'

'That's true,' said Amy. 'She must have quite a big clit to be able to see it so clearly. Do you have a big clit, Sharon?'

'Yes, Mistress,' squealed Sharon, her voice high and squeaky from her spanking.

'When do we get a go?' asked Lisa.

'What? Oh, sorry, I forgot,' said Laura, resting her hand on Sharon's bottom. 'Ohh, that's so hot, best we give her a couple of minutes. Auntie, go and stand in the corner, hands on your head, please, facing outwards I think.'

Sharon obeyed, her hands on her head thrusting her breasts out, her aching nipples bringing her attention to their erect state. Without prompting, Sharon placed her feet wide apart, exposing herself to the girls' gaze.

'You know, we should phone Heather,' said Amy.

'My sister?' said Lisa.

'Yeah, she's les, right? She'd love this.'

'True, she's with the girlfriend today, so they could both come. What do you think, Laura?'

Sharon could see Laura think it over, weighing it up, most likely the chances of her Mom taking umbrage or congratulating her for her inventiveness.

'I think that would be a great idea. They're even younger than us, and it must be so embarrassing being spanked by us, think what it will be like being spanked by a couple of eighteen-year-olds.'

'And Lesbians to boot, they will drink in the sight of your Aunt's nakedness, she's a stunner that's for sure,' said Lisa.

Sharon felt both embarrassment and pleasure as they continued to stare and comment on her body.

'Great tits,' said Amy.

'I wish I had her pussy,' said Laura. 'My lips are too flabby.'

'Hello, Heather, watcha doing?' asked Lisa, talking on her cell.

'Cool, come on over, Julie too, we're at Laura's Aunt Sharon's place. I'll text you the address. Hurry, you won't be sorry.'

'Really?' asked Amy. 'Let's see then.'

Sharon was just as curious as Laura reached under her skirt and pulled down her panties, kicking them off before raising her skirt.

'Sit down and open your legs wide,' said Lisa, putting her mobile down. 'So we can both see.'

Laura complied and suffered several minutes of exposure as, together with her friends, they discussed the pros and cons of her fleshy lips.

'You clit is quite big too,' said Lisa, boldly pushing back Laura's clit hood, exposing the throbbing bud beneath.

'As big as Sharon's?' asked Amy.

24

'Don't know,' said Lisa. 'Sharon, come over here, please.'

Sharon obeyed and, at the direction of Lisa, sat next to Laura.

'Cannot really tell for sure,' said Lisa. 'It looks bigger.'

'Sharon, get on top, facing me,' said Laura, 'so the girls can compare properly.'

Sharon obeyed and found herself looking down into the smiling eyes and grinning lips of Laura and couldn't help but smile back. Fingers pushed her hood back and tugged her clit, and, giving the soft gasp and wide eyed look on Laura, guessed they were doing the same to her, too.

'Bout the same, I'd say,' said Lisa. 'Must be a family thing.'

Laura laughed.

'Sharon's not blood, she married into the family.'

Sharon dismounted as Laura said, 'Show us yours then, if you think ours are really that big. I thought they were all that size.'

Lisa shook her head.

'No, mine's tiny in comparison,' said Amy, pulling down and taking off her jeans and panties.

As Lisa was wearing a skirt, she was already on the sofa, legs spread, as Amy climb on top, spreading her thighs wide, lowering her pussy so it was closer to Lisa's so Laura and Sharon could make an easier comparison.

There was a knock at the door.

'That'll be Heather,' said Lisa.

'Stay there,' said Laura. 'Sharon, go let them in.'

'Yes, Mistress.'

If Sharon had been surprised by the command or distressed, she hid it well as she rose and left the lounge without hesitation, returning in moments with two girls following.

'Hi, Lisa, Laura, Amy,' said Heather. 'What's going on?'

'Mom's asked us to punish Aunt Sharon,' said Laura. 'She behaved like a slut, in public no less, and you know how the family feels about that.'

Heather screwed up her face as she nodded.

'Julie, this is Laura's Aunt Sharon,' said Heather. 'The girls you know.'

Julie nodded.

'We were just comparing clits,' said Laura. 'Aunt Sharon and I have big ones, apparently.'

'So does Julie,' said Heather. 'Let me have a look.'

All eyes turned on Julie who blushed.

Heather knelt down and peered intently at Lisa's and Amy's pussies, parting their lips and pushing back their clit hoods to get a good look.

'These are normal, I'd say,' said Heather. 'Let me have a look at yours, Laura.'

Amy moved off Lisa, Laura quickly taking her place.

'Oh yes, lovely,' said Heather. 'I do like a big clit, don't I, Julie?'

Again, Julie was the focus of the group and her face went redder.

'Can we see?' asked Lisa, looking at Julie.

Julie opened her mouth, but it was Heather who answered.

'Sure, Julie, undress.'

Julie's hands immediately went behind her neck and pushed down the zip a little, then behind her back, grabbing the toggle and pulling it down all the way, allowing the thin material to pool at her feet. She was naked beneath.

'Julie is my servant,' said Heather. 'Slave in BDSM terms but the family, quite rightly, don't allow that term in case the press get hold of it. With our money it would be seized upon like a pack of wolves.'

'Same with us,' said Laura. 'Aunt Sharon is Mom's servant.'

'Really? May I?'

Laura shrugged.

Heather snapped her fingers and pointed to a spot in front of her.

Sharon's feet were moving before her brain registered her obedience to a girl almost half her age.

'Assume the position.'

Sharon placed her hands on her head, feet apart.

Heather said nothing just lifted one eyebrow.

Sharon shuffled her feet wider apart.

Heather waited.

Sharon opened herself even wider, until she felt the pull on her groin either side.

Without any preamble, Heather ran her fingers along Sharon's sex, tracing the edges of her lips before sliding down the inner surface of one.

'You are wet, aren't you?' said Heather.

Sharon nodded.

Heather smiled.

'Out loud, little one.'

'Yes, Mistress, I am wet.'

Sharon let out a soft gasp as a finger entered her.

'My my, you have a hungry little pussy don't you.'

'Yes, Mistress.'

Again, just one arched eyebrow had Sharon's mind scrambling.

'Yes, Mistress, I have a hungry little pussy.'

Heather withdrew her finger and Sharon clamped her mouth shut to bite off the moan of desire and complaint that had raced out of nowhere to her lips.

The smile on Heather's face told Sharon, she knew, causing heat to wash, head to toe, through her body.

'Julie.'

Julie was immediately kneeling by Heather's side, taking one finger into her mouth and sucking gently.

'Good girl, go sit on the couch, legs up and back so the girls can have a good look at your clit.'

'Yes, Mistress,' said Julie, moving quickly and to Sharon's thinking, eagerly, to obey.

'Oh my, she is so much bigger than Laura and Sharon,' said Lisa, running her finger along the length of Julie's clit.

'It's something special,' said Heather proudly. 'I love playing with it.'

Lisa vacated her spot so Laura could kneel, her fingers lifting it, before rolling over it.

'It's like a small dick,' said Laura.

'She squeals when I slap it,' said Heather, 'but she loves it too, bit like your servant here.'

'Come again?' asked Laura, making way for Amy.

'Sharon here, she's mortified, that's easy to see, but she's also soaking wet, which tells me her predicament is turning her on, despite believing she hates every moment. It took me weeks to get Julie to admit she was sexually aroused by the humiliations I heaped upon her.'

'We're to punish Sharon,' said Laura, 'including some inventive humiliations if we can.'

Heather looked at Sharon appraisingly as she nodded.

'I clocked the red bottom of course. Julie, what is your most humiliating task?'

'Masturbation,' Julie said without hesitation.

'Really?' asked Lisa. 'Why, we've both masturbated together before.'

Heather nodded.

'Together, yes. But under the covers, with the lights off, separate beds, except that one time and neither of us acknowledged the other.'

Lisa nodded.

'True. How is it different with Julie?'

'Julie.'

'Yes, Mistress.'

Julie rose, her face, neck and chest scarlet.

Heather cast her eyes around the room before pointing to the arm of the sofa.

Julie nodded and mounted it, spreading her thighs and lowering her pussy until it lay on the arm. Then she started to move.

Slowly at first, just her hips, then faster, her breath coming in short pants as her arousal soared. Faster and faster, her hips drove forwards and back, her pussy rubbing across the coarse wool material of the sofa.

'Mistress?' Julie raised her face and looked across at Heather.

'You may cum, servant.'

'Thank you, Mistress.'

Sharon watched, her pussy clenched tight, her breasts swollen and tender as Julie fucked the sofa, the material dark beneath her pussy lips as her arousal soaked the woollen fibres. Julie gave a soft cry as she bucked and writhed, then a louder one as she came hard, her hips grinding her pussy into the sofa arm as her orgasm crashed through her.

Heather moved across and gently stroked Julie's hair as the young girl lay panting.

'Did the material burn, my little one?'

Julie nodded.

Heather turned.

'We have leather at home,' she explained. 'The wool here would have been a little rough on my poor servant's tender bits. I am pleased, little one.'

'Thank you, Mistress,' said Julie, smiling happily.

'Time, I think, Sharon felt the sting of a spanking,' said Laura. 'Amy, if you're ready?'

Amy nodded and in no time was sitting on the sofa.

'Here, let's use this,' said Heather, moving a chair from beneath the table and placing it in the centre of the room. 'More embarrassing being over the knee proper.'

Amy nodded and switched seats before patting her lap.

Sharon placed herself over the lap silently agreeing with Heather as her head went down between her arms. This over the knee position was far more embarrassing than lying over the lap whilst they sat on the sofa.

The hand rose and fell, the sting awakening the embers of her previous spanking. After a full minute, Laura said, 'Switch to the hairbrush, Amy.'

The thwack, the solid wood made, replaced the lighter smack of her hand and soon Sharon was kicking and twisting in anguish.

'Ok, better stop there,' said Heather. 'If we're planning on all having a go.'

Amy stopped, slightly out of breath.

'We've got all day and night if we need it,' said Laura.

'Still,' said Heather, nodded her understanding. 'We want a well spanked young lady not a distraught blubbering mess, I take it. We've all been there.'

The girls nodded.

Laura looked around before nodding too.

'Mom said to make it count though,' she said.

'And we will,' said Heather. 'How about a drink?'

'Too early for wine,' said Lisa. 'Though I could do with a coffee.'

'Sharon, Julie, coffees please.'

Julie looked to Sharon, who pointed the way as she rose stiffly and flexed her back before following her out.

The Further Humiliation of Sharon
CHAPTER ONE
The Diaries

'Can I help you?'

I turn to see the shop assistant approaching Caroline.

'Yes please, can you point me to your Dominance, Bondage, and Sadomasochism section please.'

My cheeks warmed as the assistant glances my way and smiles.

'Certainly, Miss. If you would like to come this way.'

'These look interesting,' said Caroline, her hand running through a set of chains that made up a dress of sorts.

'Yes, Miss. Those are one of our favourite lines of slave wear. Would you like your friend to try them on?'

'Servant,' said Caroline. 'You can refer to her as Servant.'

'Yes, Miss.'

'I think I would like to see her in one of these.'

'The dressing rooms are right this way,' said the assistant, taking two steps, before stopping and looking back.

'That won't be necessary,' said Caroline. 'Servant, strip.'

I look at Caroline blankly, my mind trying to process what I heard clearly enough.

'Making me repeat myself will not bode well, young lady. As it is, you will be punished for your lack of alacrity.

'Yes, Miss.'

My hands tremble as they sought out the buttons of my blouse, undoing them one by one, fully aware the assistant had moved closer to watch.

Caroline's tut speeds me up and I am soon standing in my underwear, one hand over my breasts the other covering my mound.

'All of it.'

My eyes widen. I could feel them opening in disbelief. It is one thing to punish me privately, and embarrass me semi publically, but this was going too far.

'I see we need a lesson,' said Caroline, pulling a chair, miraculously and seemingly out of nowhere. 'Over my knee.'

I look wildly around me. Apart from the assistant, there were other women in the shop, browsing, though I can see them working their way closer to where Caroline had planted herself.

'I see the lesson will need to be firm. Do you have a paddle?'

The assistant nods and dashes off, only to return seconds later brandishing a wooden oval paddle.

'I assume you know how to wield that?'

The assistant nods.

Caroline looks at me.

'Would you like me to ask some of the other customers to join us or are two spankings enough to get your feet moving?'

I look around again to see the three women all looking at me, their eyes devouring my semi nudity hungrily. Without a second thought, I throw myself over Caroline's knee, embarrassment washing through me as my head drops, my hands touch the floor and my legs straighten automatically.

My bra loosens as Caroline undoes the clasp.

'Remove this, is you would.'

'Yes, Miss.'

I lift my arms as the assistant pulls my bra down my arms.

'Her panties too.'

'Yes, Miss.'

Heat washes through my body, from my toes to the tips of my hair, I swear, as the thin material is pulled off my hips and down my legs. I barely have time to process I am now naked, over Caroline's knee when the first spank lands.

The sound cuts through my thoughts. The SMACK so loud it reverberates around my head, and then the pain sets in. The second lands, then the third, Caroline giving vent to her annoyance through a rapid, hard, spanking. I didn't hold back either, giving voice to my pain with loud cries as my feet kicked and my hands curl into tight fists as my bottom blazes hotly. After what seems like an eternity but is only a matter of minutes, I hear Caroline ordering me to stand, her voice coming from a distance as I stand, my bottom stinging fiercely, only to find myself once again over the lap, my bottom once again assailed only this time by the wooden paddle.

Lost in a sea of pain, that small part of my brain flays my mind with images of the audience of women who have gathered ever closer around and the flashes of my most private parts to all as I kick and writhe over the lap of the assistant.

The beast within my core growls in pleasure as I hear Caroline say, "Keep going, she can take it," after a minutes paddling, and the comment, "Look how wet she is" which comes from one of the women looking on.

It isn't until my brain registers the pressure within my cunt, the relentless progress of fingers searching, probing deeper inside me do my senses bring my situation back to the forefront of my mind, focusing the inner eye on my present predicament.

'She's back.'

'Shame, I'm bet she was about to cum.'

'For sure.'

The beast howls with denial, moving restlessly deep within my cunt, at the very core of my sex, its pent up energy, expectant, and demanding. I barely manage to suppress a groan.

'Ladies, do not despair, my slave's punishments are far from over,' said Caroline. 'If you have the time, your presence will add value as I am a great believer shame, humiliation, and mortification make for the best punishments. This way, Sharon.'

I push myself off the assistant and stand, my legs giving a slight wobble, my cunt throbbing maddeningly, my vagina oddly empty. Heat blooms within me and radiates throughout, my face so red, so hot, a sheen of perspiration dampens my skin.

'Shaved,' a woman comments.

'I noticed that,' said another.

I so desperately want to cover my cunt at that moment.

"Cunt" the word still sends shivers through my body and mind. Such a disgusting word but one that fits me, as it heightens my awareness of my subservient position, humiliation and shame.

I give myself a shake and hurry to catch up with Caroline, fear of further public punishment tumbling my tummy over and over.

'We would like to see some of your larger dildos,' said Caroline, 'as well as Butt Plugs, clamps and pinwheels.'

'Yes, Miss.'

The assistant hurries to collect example of each, as Caroline hands me one of the chain dresses.

'Put that on.'

It takes me a few moments to work out the mechanics of how to wear the dress but soon I realise it is as simple as stepping into its midst and pulling the top most chains upwards.

As I settle the chains upon her shoulders, I ran my hands down my body, feeling the cold metal beneath. Catching my reflection within a mirror, I am amazed. I look so sexy. I feel so sexy. The chains barely cover my boobs and cunt, just enough to tantalise not scandalise.

Though it is pretty close to scandalising to warrant a second and third look. It is artfully designed.

'Sharon.'

I look around to see Caroline beckoning me with a curled finger of one hand, whilst in the other, holding a fake phallus, the proportions of which I had only seen in porn movies.

'Make yourself cum.'

I catch the tossed dildo automatically, whilst my mind once again, makes sure I am aware of the other customers, and the assistant, watching intently.

I think I have mentioned my thoughts on the difference between men and women. Whilst men, I think would have felt a tad uncomfortable at my predicament, perhaps concern over my punishments, women, not so much. Oh sure, they may be scandalised and shocked at my exhibition but this would only lead them to support my punishments, be in favour of my predicament, enjoying my humiliation at an intimate level only another woman can really fully appreciate and understand.

Caroline snaps her fingers.

My mind focuses on Caroline, locking eyes, mine pleading. Hers; cruel, wicked, sexy, and that smile, the smile that both chills and arouses me.

The beast growling draws my attention to my cunt and the realisation that I am aroused.

Abandon all hope, I think, as I spy a couch, leather, deep red, and move towards it.

Caroline moves to stand at its base, the other women shuffling to get a good spot as I lay myself down, placing one foot on the floor, the other on the couch, bent at the knee before allowing it to fall outwards, exposing myself to all.

Using my fingers, I open myself further, pulling my lips apart before placing the tip of the dildo against my opening. Fixing my eyes upon Caroline, I slowly push the dildo in, gasping as it slid in quicker than planned, its mighty head opening me up wider than ever before. Despite its girth, my vagina opens up around it with little resistance, such is my arousal. My inner muscles ripple along its length as it penetrates, going deeper and deeper within.

My lips remain open as my fingers release the fleshy folds and seek out my clit, my gasp loud as I graze my bud, followed by a whimper of need and desire.

I touch it again, my whole body jerking at the intense sensations it elicits.

Too intense. I move my fingers alongside my throbbing clit, stroking the side as I move the dildo back and forth. Slowly at first, just a little, then, as my arousal soars, so my movements became more urgent, more insistent, the thick shaft powering back and forth, slick with my feminine juices as my fingers once more touch my clit. No longer afraid of the intense spasms of erotic bliss they generate, I glory in it, rubbing my clit, stroking it, crushing it as the beast roars its orgasmic bellow and rampages through my body.

As the beast tires, slows its heaving breath sending delicious ripples through me, my own breathing echoes those pleasurable sensations until my mind calms and I open my eyes.

Heat washes anew as I see five pairs of eyes looking at me so intently, filled with desire, passion, and hunger. I cover my face with my hands and curl my legs up into my body.

'Enough of that,' snapped Caroline. 'Stand.'

I obey.

'Turn around and bend over.'

I obey.

'This one.'

My imagination plays with my mind, suggesting further punishment, anticipating the paddle, so when my cheeks are parted and cool, wet lubricant touches my smaller opening I cry out in surprise.

'Silence.'

Fingers press, and enter, sliding into my bottom, first one, then two, opening my virgin hole, my ring stinging at the intrusion.

'She's very tight, Miss.'

'Your point?'

'This plug is for the more experienced user, Miss.'

'She can take it.'

'Yes, Miss.'

My ring opens to the pressure of the plug and keeps on opening.

I cry out again as I open even further, the fear of being ripped apart teases my mind, when suddenly the pressure moves inwards in a rush, expanding my tunnel, filling me like never before. Not even the girth of the porno dildo has stretched me so. The pain is still there, stinging, aching, coupled with the heavy weightiness of the plug.

'Told you.'

'Yes, Miss.'

'Clamps.'

'We have two, Miss. These are tight, but flat, and these have less pressure but have these small teeth, see.'

'I see, nice. The tight ones on her nipples, the teeth on her cunt.'

I shuffle my feet in agitation but bizarrely the beast stirs, lifting its head with interest.

The pain in my left nipple explodes within my mind, focusing my attention to my breasts and in particular my rock hard nipples. I breathe deeply, my thoughts following the hand as it plumps my right breast, fingers seeking out my nipple, squeezing it, pinching it, before being held tightly within the jaws of the clamp. The pain is exquisite, flowing in waves, my cunt a counterpoint of pleasure. The pull on my labia captures my attention and I tense as the cold metal slowly, oh so slowly, touches my skin, then bites, the sharp little teeth pressing into my sensitive fleshy lip. The agony blazes white within my mind, an incandescent flash that leaves spots behind my eyes, followed by a second flash as my other lip is similarly bitten, chasing those spots across my vision as an orgasm ripples through my body.

'Ok, ladies, to thank you for your assistance today, my servant here will offer you her mouth or arse. You can spank her or be pleasured by her, your choice. Grab some chairs, Ladies, times a ticking.'

I remain in position, bent at the waist, my anus stretched around my plug, my nipples and labia clamped tightly, pain rippling outwards with the slightest of movement.

'Stand, servant.'

My whole body thrumming with erotic energy, I stand.

'Approach the first chair and await instruction.'

I move towards the first chair, occupied by one of the women.

'Pussy,' the woman said, pulling up her skirt and opening my thighs.

I kneel, more in automotive mode now, no longer rebelling or even thinking too much about my actions, just obeying, my mind more focused on the sensations emanating from my breasts and cunt, then what I am about to do.

Lowering my head, I place my mouth against the thin material of the woman's panties, feeling the soft folds of her pussy. My fingers glide along the woman's silky skinned thighs before ghosting over the panties and, pulling them aside, reveal her swollen lips and erect bud to my questing tongue. The woman's sigh drives me to greater efforts, slipping my tongue over the clit, flicking it, lapping it, driving the woman's arousal up, up, up until it explodes in a fan of electricity that races through her body in every direction. Holding her thighs open, I lick and suck, riding the waves of the woman's orgasm until it ebbs and eddies gently away.

Sitting back on my heels, I look up at the next woman, the shop assistant, and crawl over.

'Bottom,' she said.

I place myself over the assistant's lap, my mind lashing me with the sure knowledge she is little more than a teenager, certainly no older than early twenties. Rather than detract, this knowledge only excites the beast within, and I have to breathe to calm it before I lose control, holding it at bay, taking pleasure from my climatic denial whilst suffering the humiliation it brings.

The first spank shocks my mind, the smack igniting the smouldering embers of my recent paddling, the second, third, fourth land quickly. I know I am kicking and squirming, cries escaping as the assistant's hand lands on the base of the plug, nestled between my cheeks, driving the fattest part deeper before it's pushed back by my internal muscles, the wide girth pressing against the thin lining between anus and vagina, stroking my G spot as it moves in and out with each spank that lands upon it.

Unable to deny it any longer, I let the beast out, giving it free reign to charge from its cave and cavort and dance as it may, crying out as my body spasms, my muscles tense and release, every nerve ending firing simultaneously as my mind soars within the throes of climatic heaven. I stand with the mortifying knowledge these women have just witnessed me orgasm whilst receiving a spanking upper most in my mind.

The next two women choose pussy and I lick and suck on their clits, my fingers sliding into their pussies as I bring them to their own orgasmic delights.

Caroline is last and chooses both, bottom and pussy, spanking me hard and fast before my oral services have her crying out as her long denied orgasm is finally released.

Ordered to "assume the position" I stand, hands on head, naked, burning heat of shame and humiliation coursing through me, as the assistant nips out the back, only to return a few minutes later with coffee's for all. The customers take their ease, listening as Caroline recounts my training so far, changing their view from Caroline to me, captivated by her elicit and erotic tale.

*

Grand Mama let out her breath as Sharon closed the diary. She could feel the cooling effect of the soft breeze coming through the window upon her cunt and inner thighs, she didn't have to look down to know of her glistening skin, feminine arousal running in rivulets down her thighs. She knew this to be an exaggeration but her mind teased her mercilessly, though for sure her cunt was puffy, her lips parted, and clit visible.

'Well, that was something. I see your writing is far more descriptive then your spoken word,' said Grand Mama.

'I'd say,' said Caroline. 'I take it, you wrote that soon after we visited the sex shop, your first day of training?'

Sharon looked at Caroline, the twinkle of mirth in her eye and amusement twitching her lips only turning her on further.

'Yes, Ma'am,' said Sharon. 'I think it was the day after.'

Caroline nodded.

Kathy and Laura sat quietly, both were flushed, nipples pressed hard against their bikini tops.

'I think we could all do with some cooling off,' said Grand Mama, getting up. 'And you need a wash down before you get in my pool, young lady.'

Sharon blushed.

'Yes, Ma'am.'

Grand Mama nodded, her eyes sparkling, her lips curved in a smile as she left the room, the girls quick to follow, a dip in the pool exactly what they needed.

Caroline held back.

'I am not sure if you know, but you've brought such a change to Grand Mama. It's unbelievable,' she said, then laughed. 'I still cannot get used to calling her that, Grand Mama, it feels so wonderful to say after years of Mrs Pastors or Ma'am.'

Sharon grinned as delight suffused her body, warming her in a way the distinctly contrasted with her humiliation and shame.

'Come on, let's hose you down, then you can enjoy sometime in the pool with the rest of us.'

Sharon moved with a spring in her step. Her time at the Ranch was a heady mix of family inclusion and family pet, something that was highlighted before they had even left for their journey down.

The Further Humiliation of Sharon
CHAPTER THREE
Kathy's diary.

'Girls, wait up.'

I look behind and exchange glances with Nancy. Paula, and her two friends, Amelia and Evie were approaching.

'You girls weren't thinking about running off, right?'

'Confused, I look at Nancy and see her face redden, which sends butterflies to my tummy.

'Why would we run off?' I ask.

Paula laughed.

'Oh this is too good,' she said. 'Nancy didn't tell you, did she?'

'Tell me what?'

'That she bet a spanking in front of all the girls if she could have seven minutes in heaven with Chip.'

'What!? Well, that's got nothing to do with me,' I protest.

Paula's face was so gleeful, and I knew my fate was sealed.

'She bet for you too, if you don't pay up, neither of you are coming to my party and we will make sure everyone knows why, and we will make your life hell, you can bet on that.'

I look at Nancy, who was looking back pleadingly. Rising one eyebrow in question, Nancy begged.

'Please, how hard can it be, we've been spanked before, and we're all girls. Please, I really, really want to go.'

Any resistance flows out of me in a sigh. Nancy looked so cute, she's my best friend and I know how much she's into Chip, so... why not.

'Fine. Where?'

'Changing rooms of course,' said Paula, linking her arm through mine. 'Shall we?'

'Let me have a quick word with Nancy first,' I said, slipping my arm free.

'I cannot believe we lost,' said Nancy. Honestly, I didn't think we would.

'I cannot believe you agreed to that bet,' said I.

'It was too good to pass up,' said Nancy. 'I really want to go to Paula's party.'

'So badly we have to let Paula spank us in front of everyone?'

'Well, maybe not that bad, but close,' said Nancy.

'You owe me, big time,' say I.

I can feel my face redden as it heats up, as we enter the changing room to see all the girls in our class turn and look at me expectantly. My mind notices details as everything is sharply in focus, such as, most are naked, having come out of their showers, some in their underwear, a couple still in their short gym skirts and T-shirts, but all clearly know of the bet and the spanking to come, as every single one of them has rock hard nipples.

I can feel my mouth drop, seriously gaping open-mouthed, as Miss Kelly walks in and places her office chair in the middle of the room.

'We've not much time, Paula, before the next class arrives.'

Calm as you like.

Now, not even Nancy knows of my school girl crush on Miss Kelly and my tummy is flipping and my pussy, oh my, my pussy is so tight and wet, I could feel my orgasm building.

'Right you are, Miss Kelly,' said Paula, moving quickly to the chair, sitting and pulling me over her lap, all in one smooth motion.

I don't hesitate or resist. The idea of the next class arriving whilst I am being spanked is enough motivation to get it over and done with, not to mention the humiliation of being spanked in front of my peers. Which, as my brain lashes me with the idea, is not as bad as being seen by the next class, After all, they are all Freshmen and I'm a Senior, and nothing can be worse than being seen in such a compromising position by Freshman.

Head down, hands on the floor, my skin tingles as my skirt is flipped up, my face so hot as fingers slide under the waistband of my panties and pulls them down. I can feel many hands tugging them down my legs and off, as other hands grasped my ankles and spread my legs.

I try to close them, but to no avail, they are held firmly apart and a fresh wave of humiliation washes through me. Sure, we are all girls, but still, having ones pussy so openly displayed is usually something only ones OBGYN and boyfriend/girlfriend sees, not every girl in your class!

'Who has the hairbrush?'

'Here.'

I hang my head, not bothering to protest, accepting my fate, and willing it to be over as soon as possible.

The brush lands and I gasp as the sting warms my bottom. Again and again, the brush lands, Paula ensuring to cover every millimetre with the hard wooden surface, until it radiates with the throb of a well spanked bottom. Ordered to stand, heat burns through me as I realise my audience has grown, the Freshman class has arrived and are watching, open mouthed.

'Hands on head until we have dealt with Nancy,' said Paula. 'Amalie, Evie, got those clothes off her.'

I'm instantly pounced upon, T-Shirt up and over my head before I could even collate the thought to resist. T-Shirt held in place, my arms trapped within, I'm blind as my bra is unclasped, my breasts swinging free, and my skirt drops to my feet. Only then, are my arms freed from the T-Shirt, bra removed and I stand, naked, except for my socks and trainers, my hands held atop her head by Evie.

The sounds of spanking fills the changing room once more and all eyes are instantly drawn back to Paula, who has Nancy over her lap, bottom bared and already reddening under the brush.

My pussy tingles and tightens as I watch, conscious of the eyes that occasionally glance my way, especially those of Miss Kelly. As Nancy's bottom stings fiercely, she moves her hips, wriggling and writhing, her ankles held firmly, like my own had been, providing an unobstructed view of her pussy, which, like my own, is clearly wet, swollen, lips parted to reveal her inner charms to the watching girls.

As Nancy stands, girls pounce, stripping her naked without any such command coming from Paula. Indeed, Paula looks surprised, though happy with the outcome.

'Girls, well not you freshmen of course, you are all invited to my party, as you know, but you may not be aware that these two lost a bet, a bet that will see them naked at the party, serving food and drinks. Nancy desires seven minutes in heaven with Chip, which I have promised her, but both will provide any girl, seven minutes of heaven should they desire it.

The surprise across everyone's faces is clear to see, and in many cases, delight, though mostly disappointed faces amongst the freshmen girls.

'Ok, girls, finish up quick. Freshmen girls, get changed and out to the track, we're running today,' said Miss Kelly

Many groans met this announcement, followed by chuckles from the senior girls.

*

'I'd be quick if I were you,' said Christine, standing before her, holding her skirt up.

I look at the door, the seconds already counting down, and quickly drop to my knees.

'Make it good.'

I place my mouth over Christine's pussy, licking and sucking on the soft folds, my tongue seeking out the clitoris, desperate to finish before the door is yanked open, displaying my actions to the whole party. Christine's is not the first pussy I have given oral too, but having to lick the pussy of any girl that demands it, is as humiliating as all hell, and damned sexy too.

I wonder if that is normal or I just wired oddly?

'Ummmmm, that's nice,' Christine moans.

I'm pulled even tighter in as Christine places her hand on the back of my head.

Encouraged by Christine's soft moans, I go to town, licking, lapping and sucking harder and am rewarded with a hair pulling clench of Christine's hand upon my head, several gasps and soft cries as she comes followed by, 'Ok, ok, ok.'

As I stand, Christine pulls me into an embrace, my lips covered by hers as she kisses me passionately. Light floods the small cupboard, cries, cheers and claps greet us as we part and look out upon the revellers sheepishly, both blushing.

Stepping out of the cupboard, I smile at Nancy, who is sitting upon Chip's lap, one breast firmly gripped and fondled by the Captain of the football team.

Before the party had officially started, whilst Nancy and I were stripping down, Paula revealed, not only was we invited to the party in the first place, but that Chip had made the request of Paula, sharing that he secretly liked Nancy and wanted to ask her out.

Nancy's squeal of delight, hugging both Paula and I, seemingly unfazed by her nudity in front of us both or the prospect of being so in front of the entire senior year, which included boys! Even Paula producing her hairbrush, insisting both of us greet her guests with reddened bottoms, hardly seemed to dampen Nancy's spirits and I was so happy for my friend, I took my spanking and subsequent nude service in good spirits. The moment of abject embarrassment came, not when the first boys arrived, nor my first seven minutes in heaven, kneeling and bringing Paula off with my mouth, but when Miss Kelly arrived, my gym teacher and one I had had a crush on since she joined the school as a Teachers' Assistant two years earlier.

Everywhere I went, Miss Kelly seemed to be, always on hand, always watching, eyes drinking me in, sending heat to my face and pussy, and despite being almost sure, I wasn't sure enough to approach Miss Kelly directly, hoping, perhaps, my teacher would request seven minutes in heaven with me.

When Paula sent me to her parents' room to collect a bottle of champagne, I thought nothing of it, but when I entered to find Miss Kelly sitting on the bed, my heart pounded, and the world spun crazily.

'Are you ok?'

I found myself within Miss Kelly's arms and my whole body yearned for her touch, her caress. Having lost the power of speech, I nod, and allow myself to be guided to the bed, sitting besides Miss Kelly; leaning into her body, enjoying the soft stroking of my left arm, my teacher's arm around my shoulders.

Squeezing my thighs together, the gentle tingling intensifies nicely and a sigh slips out with pleasure. I inhale the delightful scent of perfume Miss Kelly is wearing, losing myself within the deepest blue eyes I have ever seen. My breath comes quickly now as Miss Kelly leans in. I wet my lips in anticipation, closing my eyes, lifting my mouth, my senses going wild as soft lips meet mine, her questing tongue slipping into my mouth in slow, sensuous licks. I do nothing for just a few seconds, enjoying the feel of Miss Kelly's power over me before my own ardour surges. My hands slide through her silky hair, gripping two handfuls as my arousal, so intense it is almost painful, leaps strongly. Miss Kelly moans, her breath filling my mouth, still locked together. Falling back onto the bed, my thighs part invitingly, an invite Miss Kelly accepts with alacrity, fingers finding my wet pussy, slipping between my lips, finding my opening, entering and finding my pussy hungry and demanding as it grips tightly.

My mind spins, every inch of my body totally aware of Miss Kelly's as it presses up against mine, totally owned, totally captivated by my teacher as my orgasm soars, teeters and crashes down through my body.

My cry is muffled by Miss Kelly as she kisses my lips bruisingly hard, fingers pounding my pussy, my clit crushed, rolled, and stroked, driving me to another orgasm within seconds.

Breathing deeply, I lay on my back, looking up into Miss Kelly's eyes, smiling happily.

Miss Kelly kisses the tip of my nose.

'I've been wanting to do that for so long now.'

'You shouldn't have waited,' I reply breathlessly. 'I've wanted it for even longer, Miss Kelly'

Miss Kelly leaned down and kisses me deeply.

'There will have to be rules,' said Miss Kelly.

I nod, smiling.

'And consequences.'

'What consequences?' I asked, playfully, my pussy tingling, my core tightening.

'Turn over, and I'll show you.'

I spin, giggling, so fast, Miss Kelly laughs.

'I think we understand each other,' she said.'

'Yes, Miss Kelly, I think we do.'

Kelly brings her hand down hard.

I sighed happily, wiggle my bottom, and look back at Miss Kelly.

'Spank me, Miss Kelly,' I say. 'Show me how I am to be punished should I break the rules.'

Not needing another invitation, Miss Kelly spanks my bottom very firmly indeed.

I am in heaven. Unlike my spankings from Paula or my Mom, this one is received with happiness, with eroticism and arousal and most importantly, desire; desire for Miss Kelly to own me completely.

Clearly not a novice, Miss Kelly lays down a good hand spanking, which has me squirming, kicking my legs and gasping, but never once resisting, keeping my hands firmly under my forehead.

Fingers touch the back of my thigh and I moaned, opening my legs in invitation.

A smarting smack lifts my head.

'I think you have had enough pleasure from me, young lady. I think I am due some, don't you?'

I push myself up and practically leap upon Miss Kelly, pushing her down, hands scrabbling as they push up her dress, pulled her panties to one side as my mouth assaults her sex, tongue thrusting and licking with an urgency that has Miss Kelly arching her back in orgasmic bliss within several minutes. I take my time for her next two orgasms I am determined to give her. Removing Miss Kelly's panties completely, I explore her sex thoroughly, delighting in the mind-blowing orgasms I give Miss Kelly as I examine and lick every nook and cranny of her pussy.

Finally replete, we lay in each other's arms and are happy to remain there, chatting quietly, kissing softly until Paula, who wants the house empty of revellers, chucks us out so she could go to bed.

'So your new girlfriend is one of your teachers?' said Gran Mama.

'She was, Gran Mama, but I have graduated now so no, not any longer.'

'Still, we should meet this woman and gain her measure.'

Kathy's heart raced, knowing her Gran Mama meant to spank her lover, and wondering how Miss Kelly would respond to such an idea.

'Laura, you're more a dominant, wouldn't you say?'

'Yes, Gran Mama.'

Kathy and Laura exchanged a quick glance.

Laura's hopeful and gleeful, Kathy's horrified.

'Kathy here has been away from her Mistress for far too long, I think you should give her a sisterly spanking."

'Yes, Gran Mama.'

Kathy opened her mouth, and then closed it, knowing to argue would not only prove fruitless, but no doubt only increase her punishment.

'I'd be happy to take over her Mistress's role whilst we are here,' said Laura, patting her lap as she settled herself on the edge of the bed.

'Oh, that is very nice of you, my dear. Isn't it, Kathy?'

Kathy glared at Laura before saying, 'Yes, Gran Mama, very kind.'

As Kathy laid herself over Laura's lap, Laura was quick to flip up her skirt and pull down her panties.

Hiding her head in embarrassment, she gave herself over to her spanking, stoically accepting the smacks her sister rained down.

'She writes,' said Grand Mama, reading from her diary. 'Miss Kelly spanks me most mornings, as a reminder of the rules, and I go to my classes happy, energised, and light as a feather.'

'I'll be happy to spank Kathy each morning,' said Laura. 'Report to me, naked, each morning, Kathy and I will spank you thoroughly.'

'And deny us the pleasure of watching,' said Gran Mama. 'I think not. Kathy, you will report as instructed, but downstairs, in the dining room. You can have your morning spanking before breakfast.'

'Yes, Gran Mama.'

And if I see Kathy looking down or lacking energy, I'll happily spank her then, too,' said Laura.

'Good idea. Something we can all help with I think' said Gran Mama. 'Ladies, be on the lookout and ensure our Kathy is well looked after.'

Kathy gasped and winced as Laura's hand continued to fall whilst holding the conversation with Gran Mama, surprised her Mom hadn't chimed in.

'We should let the staff know,' said Caroline.

Kathy groaned.

'I know they are all too busy but perhaps they could spare young Lisa to report any concerns.'

'Good idea, Mom, they can be incentivised by having Lisa deliver any spankings the staff feel beneficial for my little sister.'

'Yes, I like that,' said Gran Mama.

Kathy's tummy flipped at the thought of being spanked by someone younger than she, being the youngest in the family; she had never had to deal with that particular humiliation before. The idea of daily spankings sent tingles through her though, as she truly did respond positively to those her girlfriend gave her.

The Humiliation of Kathy

Chapter Two
MOLLY'S SHOP

'Let's just pop in here,' said Charlotte. 'It looks interesting.'

Kathy eyed the shop window before picking up her pace. It did look interesting.

'It's steam punk, I think,' she said, eyeing all the clothes and other merchandise.

'That's what I thought,' said Charlotte, who then laughed. 'What, you thought I was too old to recognise the style.'

'Not old,' said Kathy, 'just a little, errmmm straight.'

'Straight am I,' said Charlotte.

Kathy bumped into one of the rails of clothes sending in crashing to the floor.

'Oh my,' said Charlotte.

'Hey, what's going on?'

Kathy looked up as she tried to lift the rail, together with all the clothes still attached to see a young woman emerge from a beaded curtain, face of thunder.

'We're terribly sorry,' said Charlotte. 'My niece wasn't paying attention as usual. Head in the clouds, mooning about some boy no doubt.'

The young woman's face switched to a welcoming smile the moment she saw Charlotte and realised Kathy was not alone.

'That's quite alright Miss....'

'Grey,' said Charlotte, holding out her hand.

'Molly,' said the woman, shaking the hand firmly.

'Oh, Molly as in...,' said Charlotte waving her hand to encompass the shop.

'That's my Aunt,' said Molly. 'She's away on business, so ask me to look after the shop for her.'

'I see. A woman of many hats, your Aunt?'

Molly smiled.

'She is. Mostly import and export. This shop is more of a side line really, though we do get some really nice bits in sometimes.'

'Steam punk not for you then?'

Molly pulled a face as she shook her head.

'Naaa, nor Goth, we have a lot of that stuff here too. It's all a bit........ older, I'd say,' said Molly, looking at Kathy. 'Too old perhaps for your little one.'

Kathy straighten up, several choice remarks fighting to be first to cut this young woman down to size. Charlotte's hand on her arm stopped her in her tracks.

'Actually, I'm not looking for clothes, though I am looking for something for my niece, a hairbrush.'

'Arrhh, I can help you there,' said Molly. 'Let me just...............'

With seeming ease, Molly lifted the rail, together with clothes up right, adjusting a few of the dresses to stop them from wrinkling before turning back to Charlotte.

'If you would like to follow me to the counter we have a nice selection, I think we might even have one with sparkles.'

Kathy ground her teeth as she followed behind Charlotte.

'Come along, stop dawdling,' said Charlotte much to Kathy's amazement. She was but a step behind her.

'As you can see,' said Molly, 'we carry a limited range I'm afraid , and most have a Goth or steam punk feel to them, but all good quality. This one has sparkles,' Molly added in the hopes of sparking some interest in the selection.

Kathy's eyes lit up at the selection and reach to pick the one with sparkles.

'Don't touch,' said Charlotte smacking her hand. 'You're in enough trouble as it is.'

Molly was once again dumb struck.

Trouble, what trouble? What's going on? She thought.

'These won't do I'm afraid. The sort of hairbrush I am looking for is not for young Kathy's hair but her naughty bottom.'

Kathy felt the heat rush to her face, her mouth drop and her eyes bulge.

'What!'

'Ssssssh, child, the grown-ups are talking.'

Kathy's words didn't come as heat washed through her once again as she caught Molly's smirk.

'Arrrh, I see. Well, I think I can help you there,' said Molly, blushing herself. 'My Aunt got in a selection just a couple of months ago. We keep them out back.'

Charlotte nodded.

'It's ok, I am sure your Aunt's bottom was warmed the same way,' she said. 'I know mine was, as will Kathy's here be shortly.'

Molly nodded with a small smile of thanks for her understanding before disappearing behind the beaded curtain.

'I won't be a minute,' she called.

Charlotte spun.

'Just play along. Don't say anything out of character. Remember, you're undercover too you know.'

Kathy's mouth shut with an audible snap.

Undercover, this was part of the operation. Who is Molly and what part did she have to play?

Kathy was still mulling over this new revelation as Molly reappeared holding several boxes.

'As you can see, each one is very sturdy and fit for purpose,' said Molly.

Charlotte took each one in turn, holding it horizontally to gauge the thickness of the paddle brush, before resting it on the palm of her hand to test the size of the broad base.

'While the wooden ones are more traditional, I can attest the plastic one stings mightily,' said Molly, blushing a deeper red.

Charlotte nodded.

'I like the wooden ones best, as they leave a deeper..... impression shall we say.'

Molly nodded wisely.

'Though it is hard to know which of these four would be the best. These two are nice and thick but a little less broad than these two which would cover a nice wide area of Kathy's naughty behind.'

Hearing her name snapped Kathy out of her thoughts and she looked at the four brushes on the counter, her heart hammering in her chest as she imagined any one of them spanking her bottom. The thoughts teased her mind and her pussy tightened so hard Kathy just about managed to stifle a groan.

'What was that, dear?' asked Charlotte.

Kathy shook her head.

Charlotte tutted and turned her attention to the brushes, turning each one over.

'You could try them out,' said Molly.

'I'm sorry?' said Charlotte.

'What!' exclaimed Kathy.

'For the last time, child. Be quiet. Another peep out of you and I'll take you over my knee here and now.' Turning her attention back to Molly, Charlotte asked, 'I'm sorry, you were saying?'

'I was saying,' said Molly, 'before your niece rudely interrupted, that you could try each brush out. I know my own Mother would have turned me over her knee long before now if I acted as badly behaved as your niece has.'

Rather than be offended or outraged, Charlotte nodded in agreement.

'I have been too lenient I agree. Normally I would have given her a sound spanking by now but in these liberal times, you never know whether someone's going to report you or something.'

'I know exactly what you mean, Miss Grey. Rest assured, no one is going to kick up a fuss in this shop. My Aunt's reputation for being a strict disciplinarian is well known around these parts.'

'Well then,' said Charlotte brightly. 'I can test out these brushes and Kathy here can get what's coming to her.'

Kathy looked from Charlotte to Molly fully expecting them to burst out laughing at any moment, enjoying the shock on her face and admitting they were just having a bit of fun, after all, this was a public shop with a very large window in front.

'Why not use the bench there,' said Molly, pointing to a red leather upholstered bench. 'It's very comfy and if you are anything like Mother, which I suspect you are, you will want to take your time and ensure young Kathy here learns her lesson well.'

'Indeed. I look forwards to meeting your Mother. I think she and I will get along famously.'

'Make yourself comfy on the bench, get Kathy ready and I'll bring the hairbrushes over. Would you like a drink, tea perhaps?'

'I would love one, thank you.'

'What do you think you are doing?' hissed Kathy once Molly disappeared once again behind the beaded curtain.

'Not now,' whispered Charlotte, then louder, 'Now don't you give me any attitude young lady we're just having some fun testing the hairbrushes. Trust me you will know the difference when I tan your hide for real.'

Kathy was pulled along to the bench and as Charlotte sat down found herself steered over to one side and then over her knee. Grumbling under her breath she placed her hands on the floor. Her head jerking up as her skirt was pulled up and over her bottom, exposing her panties.

'Is that really necessary?' she asked.

'Yes, dear, now hush. We're just waiting for Molly to come back with my tea and brushes.'

Kathy was at first indignant, then as the seconds turned to minutes her position, upturned over-the-knee, skirt up, panties bared, in a shop no less played on her mind.......... and as that thought struck her she looked at the large window at the front of the shop and saw people passing by.

'There we are Miss Grey,' said Molly. 'Oh aren't they darling, cute little bunnies.'

Kathy wriggled her hips as Molly poked her right cheek.

'I'll just go close the shop,' said Molly. 'It's a little early but we've been quiet all day, then we can get started.'

'Thank you, that's alright though. Kathy is still young, so she's not bothered by others being around.'

'I understand,' said Molly, 'but best not take any chances of someone making a fuss, especially if you plan on taking those down.'

Charlotte nodded, smiling to herself as she watched Molly head to the door and turn the sign around, her hand idly stroking Kathy's panty clad bottom with one hand, her tea in the other, enjoying the scene she had created immensely. As Molly came back another wicked idea came to mind and she said,

'Could you do the honours?'

Kathy squeaked as fingers slipped under the waistband of her panties and pulled them down.

'Off?' asked Molly.

'I think that's best,' said Charlotte. 'I do so love it when she kicks, so cute.'

'Oh what a darling little kitty,' said Molly. 'Mine used to be that neat and tidy, now I've got flaps down to my knees.'

Charlotte laughed.

'Oh, come on, I bet they're not that bad.'

'Well, maybe not my knees, but they are bigger than I'd like. Thinking about getting them done.'

'No, I wouldn't. I saw a documentary on that, and this girl was in agony. They use staples you know, to seal up the cuts.'

'Ouch,' she said, one hand instinctively covering her groin, her face going white.

'So you leave your little kitty alone. It's fine, and besides, those lips of yours are no doubt super sensitive and will provide you with loads of pleasure.'

'That's true.'

'Uh hum,' said Kathy.

Charlotte and Molly laughed.

'It seems our little girl is eager to try out these hairbrushes after all,' said Molly.

'I think so too,' said Charlotte, giving Kathy's bare bottom a pat. 'Let's get started.'

'Warm up first?' asked Molly.

Charlotte made a play about thinking about that before shaking her head.

'It'll be more tender tomorrow, maybe the odd bruise but she starts her new school so a little reminder as she sits on those hard chairs won't go amiss.'

'New school? In the summer?'

'Yes, Huntingdon School for Girls. They're having a summer programme. My girl here is quite advanced academically, so I thought I'd enrolled her to keep her studies up through the summer.'

'Ohhh, that's my school,' said Molly. 'I'll be there. I can keep an eye on her for you.'

'Oh that would be lovely,' said Charlotte, not missing the wording choice and enjoying the frisson of tingles that fizzed through her body. 'See, Kathy, you've made a friend already.'

'Great,' said Kathy. 'Can we get on with it please, or better yet, buy all four and be done with it.'

Charlotte laughed.

'That's my girl,' she said before bringing down the hairbrush with a firm SMACK across Kathy's bottom.

With barely a pause, the brush was up and down again, and again and again. Indeed, for a good five minutes Charlotte spanked Kathy, enjoying the lovely wobble in her charge's buttocks and the kicks and wriggles she gave as her cheeks warmed and stung.

'Nice. Good feel to that one,' said Charlotte, holding out the brush.

Molly was quick to swap one brush for another and the spanking continued.

By the third brush, Kathy was really feeling it, her kicks and wriggles had turned quite desperate and her hand was already trapped in the small of her back.

'Last one,' said Molly. 'You are doing so well, Kathy, hold on.'

'Easy for you to say,' grumbled Kathy as she got her breath back. The knowledge there were passes -by not twenty feet away was not lost to the heat and pain in her rear, something she was venting in her "OWs! OUCHES! OOOOOHHHHHHs" and more.

Charlotte went to work with the fourth brush, enjoying the rise and fall of her arousal as she spanked away. She was truly amazed at Kathy's capacity for a spanking and the possibilities abounded within her thoughts as she brought the brush down over and over, never rushed, never slowed, never too hard, but never too soft either. Kathy's bottom was lovely and red, so red it glowed. Charlotte's pussy tightened as Kathy's pleas started.

'Oh, oh oh, come on, please Aunty, that brush is perfect; get that one, oh ooo ow, ouch.'

Charlotte finally finished. Only because she conceded that time was getting on and she'd better stop, but another wicked idea popped into her head, a small orgasm rippling through her as she enjoyed the imagery.

'Ummmmm, each have their merits but I have narrowed it down to these two,' she said, holding up the one in her hand and pointed to the second brush she had tried.

'Good choices,' said Molly. 'Nice broad backs, covers a lot of surface. Can you decide or would you like both?'

Charlotte smiled.

'Nice try, Missy. I saw the price tags on those. No, I'll only be buying one, but which.'

Charlotte tapped the brush against her lips as she pretended to consider her next move, enjoying having Kathy's soundly spanked, and bare bottom, upturned over the lap for the entire world to see as she pondered.

'I know, I need to see Kathy's face as the brushes land. Up you get, girl.'

With a smarting smack, Charlotte encouraged Kathy to her feet.

Kathy pushed herself to her feet only to be assailed by the blazing heat of her behind, sending her hopping around the shop rubbing furiously.

Charlotte and Molly shared amused grins enjoying the spectacle before Charlotte grabbed Kathy as she hopped past and propelled her towards the counter.

'Enough messing about, young lady. Bend over the counter.'

Charlotte moved around behind the counter.

'Give me your hands and keep your chin up please, I want to see the faces you pull.'

Kathy stretched out her hands and looked into Charlotte's eyes, the amused glint she could see, sending her pussy tightening and tingling.

'Molly, if you could give this naughty girl a good dozen with each, I'd appreciate it.'

'Yes, Miss,' said Molly. 'Just the two you've selected?'

Charlotte's mouth twitched, but she managed to keep her face stern.

'For now, though we might have to try out all four, to be sure.'

'Oh man,' said Kathy.

'Hush up,' said Charlotte, with a nod to Molly.

If Molly had any hesitation or uncertainty in spanking the niece of a potential customer, she certainly didn't show it in her delivery. The SMACK resonated around the shop, causing Kathy's head to shoot up and even caught Charlotte by surprise.

'Acoustics,' said Molly, delivering a second.

The word of restraint died on Charlotte's lips as she saw the sadistically wicked look on Molly's face which not only tipped her over the edge for yet another mini orgasm, it completed her mission for the day, to make a connection between Kathy and Molly. Charlotte was convinced Molly would be paying Kathy a lot of attention over the summer. The smallest twinge of guilt touched her mind, but she battered it away. Kathy could look after herself and had proven today she could take a good spanking well, very well.

Kathy's pleas brought Charlotte's focus back to the room, smiling as Kathy hopped and leapt as the brush landed over and over, her face pulling all manner of faces as the pain radiated through her petite frame.

'Very good. Next one,' said Charlotte.

*

'Happy?' asked Kathy as she clambered into the car, hissing as her bottom hit the seat.

'Very,' said Charlotte.

'Did you really need to try out all four?' asked Kathy, a bit of a whine in her voice.

'I did, I needed Molly to connect with you, and I think we managed that, especially at the end there.'

'Oh yes, Molly certainly connected with my end,' said Kathy ruefully as she shifted her weight from one cheek to the other. 'Many times.'

'Stop moaning,' said Charlotte lightly. 'Molly and I both saw the state of your pussy.'

Kathy's face burned as she covered it with her hands.

'Ohhhhhhhhhhhh,' she moaned. 'Damned body. I get so wet. I don't know why, it hurts so bad but it feels so good too.'

'Did you cum?'

'Not strongly enough,' said Kathy. 'You?'

'Same, a few small ones but the big one is waiting.'

'We need to get home,' said Kathy.

Charlotte grinned before replying,

'What's the rush?'

Kathy just gave her a look, which caused Charlotte to bark out a laugh and press her foot on the gas, sending the tyres squealing as she pulled out and drove down the road as fast as legally possible.

The Humiliation of Kathy
GYM CLASS

'Ok, Ladies, today we are going on a hunt.'

Miss Kelly paused as the girls looked at each other, some with interest, and some with undisguised lack of enthusiasm. She placed her hands on Kathy's shoulders as she surveyed the group.

'Kathy here is my niece, and she will be the hare, and you girls will be the hounds. She will be given a ten minute head start as she is quite a bit younger than you six formers, so it should make for an interesting race.'

Again, Miss Kelly paused to allow the few murmurs to die down.

'To make it even more interesting, we're going to have a wager.'

More murmurs and some shuffling of interest and unrest. The element of the unknown making some of the girls nervous.

'Any girl that fails to beat Kathy here passed the finish line will get a spanking, right here, in front of everyone, *and,*' Miss Kelly paused for dramatic effect, 'as it will be on the bare bottom, she will also walk back to the changing rooms without her skirt and panties.'

Miss Kelly paused, observing as the girls looked at each other, some whispered, some looked worried but a few looked confident, as if, even the prospect of walking back to the school half nude was no threat, no "biggy." A phrase she had heard the girls using around the school.

'And if we all beat her?' asked Cassandra, rising her hand.

'ummmm, good question,' said Miss Kelly, pausing as if thinking about it, though the smile on her lips told Kathy she was doing anything but and her tummy fluttered with nerves, though her pussy tingled deliciously. 'If you all beat her back here, then we'll have a paddle train.'

'What's that?' asked Laura-Beth.

'Well, Kathy here will bend over the end of the horse, you will split into two teams of, let's see.' Miss Kelly made a show of counting the girls in her class. 'Twelve of you, so six each side, then you move passed giving Kathy here a smack on her bottom, before joining the other team. The faster you move the more smacks you can deliver within the permitted time, switching sides with each smack.'

'How long do we get?' asked Cassandra.

'Well, two minutes?'

'I was thinking five,' said Cassandra.

Miss Kelly paused as if thinking. In truth she had been expecting and would happily have accepted ten minutes but maybe five would be best, no point tipping their one advantage to these girls, that being Kathy's capacity for a sound spanking.

'Five sounds quite a lot,' she said. 'But I'll agree to five minutes.... but.....'

Miss Kelly paused once again, really quite enjoying herself.

'Any girl that fails to beat her back here will also get a five minute spanking, each.'

'Agreed,' said Cassandra immediately.

Miss Kelly looked at Cassandra, spotting the confidence she exuded and knew she was planning on cheating. No doubt about it. Which was fine, if it brings Kathy closer to the Sixth Form girls, that's all that matters.

'Ok, Kathy, GO!'

Kathy squeaked before haring off across the field. The track was well defined, and the distance was a good two miles so it wasn't a sprint by any means, so after her initial burst, she slowed to a more steady pace, quietly confident in her ability to beat at least one of the girls to the finish line.

She heard the screams and yells of the girls as they started after her and quickened her step, the sound dropping as she entered the wooded area. Without the baying of the hounds and the peace and quiet of the woods, Kathy's pace dropped back to the steady jog that ate up the distance, silently congratulating herself and playing out the sixth form spankings in her head as she anticipated quite the show after the race.

The sound of snapping twigs and rustle of leaves was her only warning before two girls smashed into her, taking her to the ground.

'Well, hello there, cutie.'

Kathy was face down in the ground, a hand keeping there, pressing it deeper into the mud whilst another was pulling her panties down.

She struggled and tried to yell but all she managed was a muffled shout and a mouthful of mud as the first SMACK landed.

The smacks rained down on her bottom without stopping and it took a good few minutes before she became aware of the other girls running past. She struggled harder, her own spanking ordeal to come looming large in her mind.

'Steady on, girl,' came the voice. 'You'll hurt yourself.'

Kathy calmed a little.

'That's my girl. You were never going to win. Can't have some upstart youngster beating us, let alone being the cause of some of us getting a spanking. Oh no. I'm afraid it's the paddle train for you. No grassing now, we don't like grassers.'

Kathy felt the weight lift from her head and she pushed herself up, spitting out mud and leaves before turning, looking up to see Cassandra and Laura-Beth.

'What's a grasser?' she asked.

Cassandra raised an eyebrow in surprise, more expectant of outrage and anger then calm considered questioning from the young teenager.

'Someone who tells, duh,' said Laura-Beth.

'Oh, a snitch,' said Kathy, sitting up. 'I'm no snitch.'

'Good to know,' said Cassandra. 'Now you be a good girl and count to one hundred and then finish the race, we should all be well back by then.'

Kathy nodded.

'Oh,' said Cassandra, as Laura-Beth tore off at a ran. 'We're going to suggest to Miss Kelly we get to spank you for the same amount of time it takes you to get back.'

'You think you can run the remaining distance more than five minutes faster than me? We're at least half way, more I'd say,' said Kathy.

'We are, but then I didn't say I was the marker. No, Shelly has already suggested the change in the rules, and she should have made it back by now. She's really fast and knows the shortcut.'

Kathy jumped to her feet.

'Ah, ah, ah. Count to one hundred. I'll know if you cheat too. Anything less than a twelve minute train and you'll be for it later. You get me?'

Kathy nodded, her mind spinning at the thought of a twelve minute spanking from twelve girls, though the symmetry made her smile. The girls obviously liked to keep things simple.

Cassandra looked at Kathy appraisingly, reassessing her initial thoughts until it dawned on her, Kathy was already counting.

'Oh, you little minx,' she said with a laugh.

Kathy smiled and gave a mocking wave.

Cassandra felt her own tummy flutter. She was not the fastest of the girls and the thought of going over Miss Kelly's lap for a spanking, in front of all her friends sent tingles throughout her body and made her pussy clench. She had been in charge for so long, she had grown used to being in control so these feelings were somewhat of a surprise, and not totally unwelcome. Still, she wasn't about to experiment in front of everyone, so she turned and hot footed it. Running for all she was worth.

As she burst out of the woods, she could see the girls all standing together, watching, waiting, when all of a sudden they started screaming and pointing. Looking over her shoulder she saw Kathy emerge from the woods, determination set upon her face. Cassandra put her head down, pumped her arms and lifted her knees to force every ounce of speed from her frame. Paying attention to her gym teachers all those years paid out in the end as she narrowly crossed the finished line ahead of Kathy but it was scarily close.

Miss Kelly pressed the button on her stop watch. '12 minutes 5 seconds,' she declared. 'We'll round that up to 13minutes.'

Even as winded as she was, Cassandra looked up in surprise.

Wow, she really doesn't like her niece, she thought.

This thought was further strengthened when Miss Kelly declared she was so disappointed in her niece, she would take her spanking totally nude *and* walk back to school the same way.

All the girls were shocked, and the murmurs rippled around the group.

'Off with everything,' said Miss Kelly.

Kathy looked pleadingly towards Miss Kelly before huffing with resignation and pulling her top off. Small breasted, she often went without a bra so was instantly naked above. A quick shove down of her skirt and panties and she totally naked.

'Over the end of the horse,' Charlotte barked, pointing to the vaulting horse the girls had lugged all the way from the gymnasium, its purpose now crystal clear.

Two girls helped Kathy up as it was so tall, Kathy's legs dangled down, feet inches from the ground.

'Two teams!'

The girls shuffled into two teams of six.

'Ok, you have 13 minutes to lay as many spanks as you can across my lazy nieces bottom. Anyone that decides to go easy will take her place and we will start again.'

'Miss, we are running dangerously close to being late for our next class,' said Brenda.

'Then I wouldn't waste any more time,' said Miss Kelly, lifting her stopwatch, placing her whistle in her mouth, blowing it hard and then pressing the button.

Cassandra and Laura-Beth were the two group leaders, and they ran passed Kathy almost on par, each delivering their smarting SMACK, SMACK

The rest of the girls followed their lead.

SMACK, SMACK.

SMACK, SMACK.

SMACK, SMACK.

SMACK, SMACK.

SMACK, SMACK.

As they ran around and went again, each girl was now smacking the other cheek, ensuring an even delivery throughout, and on it went.

Kathy was stoic to start with, taking the spanking in her stride. The heat and sting a pleasant counterpoint to that within her pussy, replacing sting with tingles of course. Being bullied by girls was one of her biggest fantasies so this whole experience for her was one of erotic bliss, not that it wasn't proving challenging too. Her humiliating spanking in the school's square was something that still made her blush hotly whenever she thought about it.

By the eighth minute, Kathy was kicking and writhing atop the vaulting horse, by ten she was giving voice to every spank that landed, and by twelve her bottom was on fire.

'One minutes, girls, pick up the pace.'

The girls obeyed, already breathless, hot and sweaty, their hands smarting from the smacks they had already laid down. But fearing Miss Kelly's threats of taking Kathy's place and starting over, they landed their SMACKS with all the force they could muster.

The piercing sound of the whistle brought the train to a halt and Cassandra and Laura-Beth quickly went to Kathy, helping her stand, giving her bottom a rub. Though, for all their concern, they couldn't help join the laughter as Kathy leapt into the air, breaking free from their offering hands and rubbed her bottom furiously and then danced around hopping and skipping as her held her deep red bottom.

'Off to the showers with you,' said Miss Kelly. 'You four, take that horse with you.'

The girls she had singled out groaned as they watch the other girls' race off.

*

Kathy was soaping herself when the curtain behind her was pulled opened and Cassandra entered her shower cubicle.

'Hey!' said Kathy, covering her boobs and her pussy with her hands.

'Quiet, Brat,' said Cassandra, slapping away her hands and pushing her up against the wall. 'Let's see what we are dealing with.'

With her feet, she kicked Kathy's legs apart before pressing one hand between her thighs, fingers slipping easily into Kathy's pussy.

'Ummm, despite the treatment you have received today you are soaking wet, or maybe because of it? Open.'

Kathy opened her mouth and dutifully sucked on the slick fingers Cassandra pushed into her mouth.

Beyond Cassandra, she could see Laura-Beth and the other girls, and she blushed.

Cassandra's eyebrow shot up.

'But easily embarrassed I see.'

Spinning Kathy around, Cassandra grabbed both her cheeks in her hands and squeeze, causing Kathy to hiss and rise on tip toe.

'So you certainly felt that spanking then, I was beginning to wonder.'

Cassandra turned Kathy around and lifted her chin so she was looking directly into her eyes.

'You are one to watch, I think,' she said. 'Wash me.'

'What?' asked Kathy, confused at the sudden switch.

'Wash me, don't me make ask again.'

Kathy grabbed her scrub and began to lather it.

'No, silly. With your tongue.'

Kathy placed the soap and the scrub down and started to kiss and lick Cassandra's boobs.

Cassandra stopped her by placing her fingers once again under Kathy's chin.

'Soap me first and then lick it off.'

Kathy's face made Cassandra laugh.

'Now you're getting it.'

Cassandra raised her hands above her head, scooping up hair and holding it atop her head as Kathy lathered up the soap in her hands and rubbed it over Cassandra's body.

Cassandra let out a soft moan in response.

'Don't take all day,' she murmured.

Kathy picked up the pace, kneeling to soap Cassandra's legs up to her thighs, then between. Cassandra turned around and Kathy soaped her bottom. Cassandra leaned forwards. Enough of a command for Kathy so soap between her cheeks before spreading them wide apart and licking the suds out, ensuring the tip of her tongue delved deep into Cassandra's opening.

'Good girl, quick now.'

Kathy lapped the thick soapy suds from Cassandra's bottom, then from her legs. Turning Cassandra, she completed the front, flicking her tongue rapidly between the thighs to both clean and pleasure before working up her body.

Standing, she flicked her tongue over Cassandra's breasts before standing back.

'Good job,' said Cassandra, touching Kathy on her nose. 'Ok girls,' she said, turning around. 'Show's over. Get dressed and onto the next class.'

The girls hurried to their lockers.

'Normally I'd make you wait and arrive late so we could watch you get a spanking, but I think you have had enough for one morning. Get dry and get dressed quick.'

Kathy nodded and grabbed her towel, hurrying to her locker.

Humiliation: The Beginnings Book One.
CHAPTER THREE
THE MOTHERS

'Mum?'

'Hello, Georgina.'

'Come on in,' said H. 'All of you.'

The door opened fully and the three slaves entered, Georgina leading the way, Cathy next with Sally looking over Cathy's shoulder, too curious to wait the two seconds to see Georgina's, Cathy's and her own mother sitting in the large living room with their Master, H.

'Mum?' said Sally.

'I'm sorry, Mum. We would have dressed had we known,' said Georgina, her stance awkward as she covered her boobs and pussy with her hands. 'Harold is the new owner of the estate and is unfamiliar with our ways.'

Georgina's mother laughed.

'Look at our girls,' she said to the other Mums. 'To think we used to wipe their kitties and powder their bottoms and now they're embarrassed for us to see them naked.'

H smiled. It was true. All three girls were covering themselves, blushing and backing slowly to the door.

'Stand still, ladies, hands by your sides,' said H.

The three girls looked like rabbits caught in headlights as they instantly obeyed, their eyes wide and wild as they tried to get ahead of what was happening.

'I see my girl has gone without hair,' said Georgina's mum.

'Oh, she didn't shave it as a teen, Phoebe?'

Phoebe shook her head.

'Wasn't in vogue back then,' said Phoebe. 'You can really see everything.'

'No!'

Everyone jumped.

'Georgina,' said H sternly added.

Blushing, Georgina inched her feet wider apart.

'That made me jump,' said Phoebe.

'Me too. Leonie, how about your child?'

Leonie nodded.

'Cathy shaved the moment hair started to grow,' she said. 'She was very pussy proud, actually.'

Rachel laughed.

'My girl was totally pussy obsessed,' she said. 'I caught her watching porn when she was what, ten? She flipped out as her pussy changed and her labia grew, demanding no less then to have her labia changed.'

'Can you do that?' asked Leonie.

Rachel nodded.

'Labiaplasty or some such. I said no, of course. I showed her mine and both her elder sisters to prove hers was totally normal and then strapped her pussy every time she brought it up after that.'

Did she accept that?

Rachel shook her head.

'So what did you do?'

'I took a photo of it and put it on a website and asked for people to rate it out of ten. It scored 9.7.'

'And she was convinced?' asked Phoebe.

'Finally, yes,' said Rachel.

All three mums looked at Sally, or more specifically they looked at her pussy.

Sally's face went red.

'Come closer,' said Rachel.

Sally inched forwards.

The mothers laughed.

Rachel exchanged glances with H, who nodded.

'Come closer, child. So we can have a good look.'

Sally moved as if her feet were made of lead, but it wasn't that far and within moments she was standing in front of her mum and two other women, all of whom were looking at her pussy.

'Turn around, bend over,' said Rachel. 'Give us a better look.'

Sally groaned but obeyed.

'See, perfectly normal,' said Rachel, her fingers running along Sally's labia, before pulling the lips apart, displaying her most intimate openings to all.

'Mum,' whined Sally.

'Hush,' said Rachel.

'She gets wet like my girl,' said Leonie.

'And mine,' said Phoebe. 'Georgie, come here.'

George obeyed though her face flushed red, and she too, found herself bent at the waist, presenting her pussy to her mum and the other mums, making an odd whine as her Mum opened her pussy lips.

'Oh my, she is wet,' said Leonie.

'When she was a kid, I had to spank her she got so wet. I couldn't let her Dad spank her like her brother and sister. Too embarrassing.'

'For Georgina.'

'For me,' said Phoebe.

'I was the same,' said Rachel. 'Especially when she started to orgasm.'

'Mum!'

'Hush I said.'

Rachel slapped Sally's pussy.

'Ow.'

'She would orgasm over your knee?' asked Leonie.

'Yep, I'd spank her all the harder but knew I had to come up with something else, so I spanked her in front of her sister, and her friends.'

'Did that work?' asked Phoebe.

'Not really. My thighs were soaked and I swear she had multiple orgasms, disguised by her spanking induced lap dance.'

'Cathy, come over here.'

Cathy moved, assuming the same position as the other girls without command, parting her thighs wide.

'Were you the same, Cathy? Did you come whilst I spanked you?'

'Sometimes, yes.'

'Georgina?'

'Yes?'

SLAP!

'OW. Yes, yes I would orgasm whilst over your lap,' said Georgina.

'And after,' said Phoebe. 'You always masturbated after I spanked you, didn't you?'

'Yes, Mum.'

'What do you say, ladies? Shall we get this show on the road?' asked Phoebe.

'I cannot wait.'

'Me neither.'

'Over my knee Georgina,' said Phoebe.

'Mum, no!'

Phoebe laughed.

'Let's do this one at a time,' said Leone. 'Phoebe, take their chair in the middle of the room. I suspect Howard placed it there for this specific purpose.'

H nodded and smiled.

'Ok, then,' said Phoebe. 'Georgina, follow me.'

Phoebe took Georgina's ear and led her, still half bent over to the chair, sitting and guiding Georgina over her lap all in one move.

'Oh wait, stand, young lady.'

Georgina stood, and Phoebe stood and shimmied out of her skirt.

'Save it getting wet,' she said, laughing.

The other mums laughed.

H looked at Phoebe with sexual interest. All young mums, Phoebe was the eldest at 58, Leonie was 47 and Rachel was 38. Their daughters inheriting their looks from their mothers as well as their figures.

'You know, and say if I am speaking out of turn, but looking at these cute young bottoms I wouldn't mind spanking one of your girls, in exchange for you spanking mine,' said Rachel.

'I was thinking the same thing,' said Leonie.

'Me too,' said Phoebe. 'But my idea was that we each spank each girl, starting with our own.'

'Oh yes, that's a good idea,' said Rachel.

'I like it to,' said Leonie. 'And tell me if this is too weird, but I am kind of curious as to whether the girls all masturbate the same way.'

'So we have them masturbate afterwards, you mean. Just to see.'

Three exclamations of "Mum!" filled the room.

The mothers chuckled.

'Sally, go stand by the wall,' said Rachel.

'You too, Cathy,' said Leonie.

Both girls obeyed, automatically placing their hands on their heads as they faced the wall.

Rachel, Leonie, and Phoebe exchanged glances before turning to Howard.

'Well trained.'

'I cannot claim credit,' said Howard. 'Their previous Master's work.'

'Still can't get used to my girl being a sex slave,' said Phoebe. 'She was always so fiercely independent.'

'I was surprised too,' said Leonie.

'Not me,' said Rachel. 'Once we knew our Sally was submissive, we encourage it and arranged for her to come here.'

'This is going to be an educational weekend,' said Phoebe.

'And interesting,' said Leonie.

'And fun,' said Rachel. 'Don't forget the fun.'

The women chuckled.

'Talking of which. Since we have all weekend, we don't need to rush things,' said Howard.

'We could spank each of our daughters,' said Rachel, 'and perhaps then take a tour of the estate?'

'I was thinking we could have the girls show us how they masturbate,' said Phoebe. 'I have to confess to having a curiosity.'

Leonie nodded, though blushed.

'I was wondering that myself but would never have had the nerve to voice it.'

Rachel laughed.

'Well, I know how Sally masturbated as I taught her how.'

'Really?' asked Phoebe.

Rachel nodded.

'Is that weird?'

'Kind of, yeah,' said Leonie, her smile broadening to a chuckle.

Phoebe nodded, laughing.

'How exactly did you show her?' asked Leonie.

'I showed her how I did it,' said Rachel. 'I did the same with her older sister.'

'I used to watch Georgie,' admitted Phoebe. 'Though she didn't know.'

'Mum!' said Georgina.

'Seriously, you didn't want an audience? You always left your door open. Just a crack, but enough to see.'

'So we each spank our daughters. After each spanking, they show us how they masturbate. To orgasm?'

'Only fair,' said Rachel.

'I agree,' said Phoebe. 'Then they can show us around the estate.'

'We can give them their second spankings after lunch,' said Leonie.

'And they can masturbate using one of the other girl's techniques,' said Rachel.

'Are we getting a bit carried away?' asked Phoebe?

'Isn't this the sort of thing the girls came here for?' asked Leonie.

'It is,' said Rachel. 'Just stick to the two girls not your daughter and it'll be fine.'

'I can do that,' said Leonie.

'Georgina?'

'Yes, Mum.'

'Is this what you girls want?'

'Yes, Mum.'

'Naughty girls,' said Phoebe, bringing her hand down smartly across Georgina's bottom.

Georgina wriggled her bottom, glad the spanking had finally started. Being over her mum's knee whilst she discussed masturbation of all things was totally surreal and embarrassing. The thought of masturbating in front of her mum sent heat washing through her. She winced as the hand fell again.

Georgina spared a glance at the two other mothers, both of whom were taking their ease, sipping tea of all things as they watched with keen interest, smiles playing across their lips.

Another spank brought Georgina's attention back to her smarting cheeks.

Phoebe was enjoying herself, which made her slightly guilty and thrilled at the same time. Her hand rose and fell onto the softness of Georgina's cheeks. It had been so long since she had last spanked her daughters. When Howard phoned her; she jumped at the chance and had been masturbating furiously the two days she had to wait until she had arrived at the Manor House.

Georgina twitched and soft cries laced her breathing.

'Now we're getting somewhere,' said Leonie.

Phoebe shared a smile with her new friend, her hand never faltering. It all came back the instant her hand had fallen for the first time. How Georgina would twitch, soft cries giving way to louder ones as her feet would lift, one at a time at first, then together as they kicked, her hands balled into fists. Phoebe smiled as Georgina's foot lifted off the ground.

By the time she was kicking, Phoebe was despairing, her arm aching and her hand stinging.

'Nearly there,' she said, more to herself than her audience, who showed no signs of boredom as the spanking went on for a further two minutes before Phoebe paused.

'Wow, ok that took a lot longer than it used to.'

'Perhaps we should use the hairbrushes,' said Leonie.

'You brought yours?' asked Phoebe.

'Of course,' said Leonie.

'I was thinking we could use those tomorrow,' said Rachel, 'together with the strap.'

'That makes sense,' said Phoebe, 'and I'm not complaining, just saying.'

The mums nodded.

'Ok, Georgina. Show time,' said Rachel, clearly excited.

Georgina and Phoebe blushed.

'Oh this must be good. Look, they are both blushing,' said Leonie.

'Best get to it, girl,' said Phoebe.

Georgina nodded, standing, then kneeling.

'She would normally do this in front of a mirror,' said Phoebe.

Knees part, one hand between her thighs the other behind her head, Georgina stroked her pussy, rolling her clitoris beneath the pads of her fingers, her arousal, already simmering, began to boil, leaping up only to fall back into the pool, bubbling away only to leap up again.

'Both hands,' said Howard.

'That's right,' said Phoebe. 'I'd forgotten that.'

112

Georgina slid her other hand between her thighs from behind, fingers seeking, finding and entering her pussy, as the other picked up speed, rubbing faster, harder, her hips moving back and forth, breath coming in gasps and pants. When she came, she cried out, both hands moving in unison, not stopping until she cried out again.

'Two,' said Leonie, conversationally.

'I don't think she'd done yet,' said Rachel.

'Oh my God,' cried Georgina as she cried out a third time, louder and longer than the other two together.

Collapsing to the floor, Georgina gasped and panted.

'Wow,' said Leonie.

'I'm jealous,' said Rachel.

'I'm turned on,' said Rachel.

All eyes turned to her.

'Too much information?'

Rachel chuckled.

'No, never. Not between us, agreed?'

'Agreed,' said Leonie.

'Agreed,' said Phoebe.

'My Sally can take care of you. Sally.'

Sally turned, moving to Phoebe and kneeling before her.

'Really?'

'Really,' said Rachel.

'Yes, Ma'am. I would be happy to serve,' said Sally.

Phoebe looked to Howard.

'I assume you're staying.'

'I am,' replied Howard.

Phoebe looked around at the faces watching before nodding.

'Ohhh goodie,' said Rachel.

Sally slid her hands along Phoebe's thighs, sliding her fingers into the waist band of her knickers, gently tugging.

Phoebe lifted her hips, allowing them to be drawn down her legs and off.

With gentle pressure, Sally parted Phoebe's thighs, placing a kiss on the lushes lips that nestled between, eliciting a soft sigh. A sigh that soon became a gasp, a soft cry, then a louder one, then a full throated scream of pent up release that was so intense her whole body went into spasm.

Sally sat back, smiling. Phoebe leaned forward, placing a kiss onto Sally's lips.

'Thank you, my dear.'

Phoebe stood, laughed, and sat back down.

'Legs wobbly.'

Everyone laughed.

'More tea?' asked Howard.

'Oh yes,' said Phoebe. 'Mine must be cold by now.'

'Georgina, if you have sufficiently recovered perhaps you could do the honours. Cathy, I think it's you turn over your Mum's lap.'

Leonie stood, undoing the buttons on her trousers, pushing them down and taking them off before taking her seat on the chair.

'Come, Cathy.'

Cathy moved from her place on the wall, working her neck which had gotten a little stiff looking over her shoulder for so long before placing herself over her Mum's knee, all her childhood spankings flooding back as she took the familiar position. Her spanked took as long as Georgina's and she kicked and writhed, squealed and cried out wonderfully as Georgina served tea to her Mum and refreshed Rachel's and Howard's cups. Once finally replete, Leonie bade Cathy to stand, chuckling as she hopped and rubbed her bottom, as she looked about the room.

'Lost something?' asked Phoebe

Cathy shook her head, blushing as she moved to a chair with padded arms and pulled it into the centre of the room. Looking at Howard, she mounted the arm at his nod, pressing her pussy against the cushioned padding. Her hips moved slowly at first, rubbing her pussy against the fabric, picking up speed as her arousal mounted. Everyone watched as Cathy gave herself over to the climax that was raging within her. As it exploded free, she threw her head back and cried out, her hips riding the cushioned arm back and forth as orgasm after orgasm erupted, spreading throughout her body in a tingling, surging rush that left her gasping for air, crying out again as the next came just as fast, just as hard.

'I'm going to have to try that,' said Phoebe.

'Me too,' said Rachel.

'Is that why the arms of my sofas are so dark?' said Leonie. 'You little minx.'

Cathy blushed as she swung her leg over the arm of the chair and stood, gently stroking her pussy.

'Hands on your head, girl,' said Leonie. 'I think you've had enough.'

Cathy smiled as she moved her hand away.

'Ok, Sally, our turn,' said Rachel, moving to the chair.

Sally skipped over to her Mum, kissing her on the cheek before settling herself over the lap.

Rachel spanked with a steady pace, covering both cheeks and the backs of Sally's thighs, eliciting higher pitched cries than those across her bottom, only encouraging Rachel to return to the sensitive area time and time again. By the time Rachel allowed Sally to stand, her bottom and thighs were red to just above the backs of her knees.

'Thorough,' said Leonie.

'Very,' said Phoebe.

'The girl took it well,' said Leonie.

Phoebe nodded.

'Show time,' said Leonie, as Sally lay on the floor, her feet towards the mums as she shyly parted her thighs wide, both hands sliding between one opening her lips, the other rubbing her clit rhythmically. As her arousal mounted and surged, her hips left the floor, her fingers pressing harder against her clit, the other hand delving lower, fingers entering, thrusting as her breath came in gusts laced with soft cries and moans. When she came, her cries barely rose higher, her body shaking, hips jerking before she slowed her movements and then stopped, smiling shyly as she sat up.

'Very nice, dear,' said Rachel, stroking the top of Sally's head.

Rachel returned to her original seat as the three girls stood in a line, hands on head, waiting as their mum's sipped their tea.

'Turn,' said Phoebe.

The girls turned, withering in embarrassment as their mum discussed their spanked bottoms and backs of thighs in Sally's case, not to mention the amount of pussy they each showed from behind, debating the level of arousal necessary to swell the lips to the extent each girl displayed.

'Time for the tour,' said Phoebe, placing her cup down.

'Oh yes, lets. Howard, are you ok if our girls show us around?'

'Of course. I'll be in my study if you need me.'

Howard stood as the girls linked arms with their Mum's, walking them out, taking turns to talk about the House, telling tales of ghosts, murders, lost treasure, loves, elicit affairs and more.

Smiling to himself, Howard entered his study, turning on his computer monitor which showed the living room, now empty. Pressing a few buttons, the room became occupied by the three slaves and three mothers. Smiling, Howard burned three copies, marking each, Phoebe, Leonie, and Rachel.

Humiliation: The Beginnings Book One.
FOURTH SPANKING

Tracey smiled at the face that popped around the door.

'Simone. You're as lovely as you look on the computer.'

'Thanks, come in, come in.'

The head disappeared and the door opened wide.

Curious Tracey and Victoria exchanged glances before stepping into the hallway.

'Oh, I see,' said Victoria, hugging a naked Simone.

'Yeah, Mum's naked too.'

'You started without us I see,' said Tracey.

'Things have gotten a little ahead of plan,' said Simone. 'We were hoping you'd be here a little earlier.'

'I know, I'm sorry. Traffic was a nightmare,' said Tracey.

'You know Philip will spank you both for tardiness though, right.'

'Counting on it,' said Victoria.

'Cool. You've got to strip.'

'What?'

'Strip. Take off all your clothes.'

'Seriously?' asked Tracey. 'It's not like we really know the man or anything. And it's the first time we're meeting in real life.'

'Yeah, I know. It's all a bit rushed. Not like how we planned it. Events have gotten a little ahead of themselves.'

'Tracey, Victoria, I'm so glad you made it. I was beginning to worry you'd had cold feet.'

'Maggie, how lovely to finally meet.'

'Forgive the lack of clothing. Things have gotten away from us this morning.'

'So Simone was saying. We have to strip as well?'

'Yes, if you would. You'll see why in a minute. Philip's orders.'

'Come on, Mum,' said Victoria, already down to her underwear. 'It's what we signed up for, after all. If a little quick. There'll be four naked girls and one clothed man. How bad can it be?'

Maggie and Simone exchanged quick glances before schooling their faces to total innocence.

'Where should I put these?' asked Victoria.

'Come on, I'll show you our room,' said Simone.

'Cool.'

Victoria and Simone raced upstairs, Simone's bottom almost glowing is was so white compared to Victoria's.

'We need to try out that nudist camp,' said Maggie.

Tracey smiled as she shrugged out of her blouse.

*

The girls came thundering down the stairs within moments. Victoria taking her Mum's hand as they follow Maggie and Simone into the lounge.

'Ohhh,' gasped Tracey as she entered the room to find not just Philip but Liane and Jackie sitting there, calmly drinking tea, their eyes flickering from one naked girl to the other as they formed a line.

'Good, we are all here, finally.'

'I'm sorry, Sir,' said Tracey. 'Traffic.'

'You didn't take traffic into account when planning when to leave.'

'I did, but.....'

'Not clearly enough.'

'No, Sir.'

'Sixty four minutes by my reckoning.'

'Yes, Sir.'

'So by your punishment regime, that's six four spanks, am I right?'

'Yes, Sir.'

'Each.'

Phillip looked to Victoria as he said that.

'Yes, Sir,' said Victoria.

'Take your positions on the bench.'

Victoria and Tracey looked at two wooden benches before them.

'Bend over them?' asked Tracey

'Straddle them.'

'Oh.'

Both girls straddle the benches.

'Jesus, I can see everything,' said Liane.

'Yes, Maggie and I worked hard on these. It took several versions to get the width of the bench wide enough to display everything, yet be possible to straddle somewhat comfortably for a lengthy period and judging by the red faces, or redder faces would be accurate, both Tracey and Vicky are feeling the humiliation intended in being exposed in such a manner.'

'I bet,' muttered Jackie.

'Let's make sure they know exactly how much they are showing,' said Philip, snapping a couple of shots on his phone. 'Perfect for our group profile as well.'

'Group profile?' asked Liane.

'Yes,' said Maggie. 'Tracey, Victoria, myself, and Simone are joining Philip in an.... extended family relationship.'

'Polyamorous,' said Vicky.

'So this profile would be on some sort of fetish site?' asked Liane.

'Yep,' said Maggie. 'It's how we all met.'

Tracey groaned and covered her head after looking at the photo Philip took. Victoria's face was already glowing hotly.

'Can they get up?' asked Liane.

'If they want to. Tracey, Victoria, would you like to stand, get dressed, leave even?'

'No, Sir.'

'No, Sir.'

Liane nodded.

'I've never seen one, let along two from this angle,' said Liane. 'If her vagina opens any more I'll see her cervix.'

'We have speculums on order to achieve that,' said Maggie.

'You want that?' asked Liane calmly.

'Humiliation. It's a tradition Tracy and I grew up with and have been introducing our daughters too, within their punishments. Now we're all adults we have collectively been seeking out a Head of House with the creativity and imagination to deliver.'

'And he's the best you could come up with?' asked Liane. 'No offense.'

'Oh offense taken,' said Philip, though he winked, throwing away the insult before it could upset the delicate balance.

Maggie laughed.

'He's not so bad looking, cute in a way. You have to spend a little time with him for the physical attraction to kick in. It's his mind that will grab you first. This is all his idea.'

Liane switched her gaze from Maggie back to the two women straddling the benches, their openings, all three, clearly visible.

'They're both wet,' whispered Jackie.

'I noticed that too,' said Liane. 'No doubt they are both horribly humiliated and completely aroused by it. Vicki has a lovely fat little clit, did you see. Just like yours.'

'Mum!'

Liane laughed.

'This was your idea, Jackie and, if we stay, I suspect we will be straddling those benches ourselves before the weekend is out, so everyone will see for themselves.'

Jackie looked to the two girls again, her face blushing.

'Philip, we should proceed with the girls' punishment. Actually Liane, we were thinking of introducing you to our lifestyle a little more gently than this, so I can fully appreciate you may want to leave.'

Liane smiled as she sat back, picking up her mug of tea.

'I'm grateful you think enough of our friendship to include me. I'm happy to participate. Jackie?'

'Me?'

'You're of age. You get to decide for yourself. You can see, quite explicitly I might add, your immediate future if you choose to stay. Your choice.'

Jackie looked at the two women, more, the two pussies so openly displayed, not to mention the sixty four smacks they were both going to receive that were sure to smart.

'I'm in,' she said.

Philip moved to stand next to Victoria.

'Why were you late? As a matter of interest?'

'Mum couldn't decide what to wear.'

'Vicky!'

'It's true.'

'Snitch.'

'I am not.'

'You just did.'

'Oh, right.'

Everyone laughed. Laughter that died quickly as the sound of the crisp SMACK! filled the room, followed by an "ouch."

The hand fell slowly, about once a second, each smack landed on an alternative cheek.

The whispered count caught their attention.

'Keep going, Jackie. A little louder so the girls know just how many they have left.'

'Thirty four. Thirty five.'

The squeals, Ows and Ouches accompanied each SMACK delightfully.

'Sixty Three, Sixty Four.'

'Now Tracey here as had to lie here, waiting her turn, hearing the spanking she is about to receive. A torture of itself I think.'

Tracey nodded.

'Ready?' Asked Philip.

Tracey shuffled a little but there was no respite, her position was dictated by the bench, broad enough to stretch her thighs wide, high enough her knees couldn't reach the floor, her weight supported by the bench.

Philip moved from her head down towards the business end, delivering the first of the sixty four spanks. Same pace, same intensity as those he had given Victoria.

Punishment complete, both girls stood, rubbing their bottoms, their eyes down, mortified at the darkened wood of the benches.

'Tea?'

Tracey looked up surprised.

Maggie laughed and hugged her friend

'Still has to be fun, right?'

Tracey laughed.

'Let's go to my room,' said Simone, taking Vicky's hand. 'Jackie.'

Jackie leapt to her feet and moved quickly, taking Vicky's other hand and together the three of them left the room.

*

'Feels odd, sitting here naked with you dressed,' said Vicky.

Jackie nodded.

'I was thinking the same, only I felt off being dressed whilst you two are naked. You both seem so relaxed.'

'It gets easier,' said Simone. 'Though there's these odd moments when I suddenly become self aware, get all shy and hot, you know.'

'I've not been naked as long as you I assume,' said Vicky. 'But yeah, that's how I feel. Especially now, just us. Even in front of the mum's it's embarrassing, but Philip. Vicky shivered and hugged herself.

'That bad?' asked Jackie.

Vicky shook her head.

'Not bad. More embarrassing, when my brain reminds me I'm naked. And exposed like that, you know, just now. So humiliating.'

'But a turn on, right?' said Maggie, walking into the room.

'Yeah,' said Vicky. 'Ohh thanks. I'm parched.'

Maggie placed the tray down.

Simone laughed.

'Chocolate biscuits?'

'Special weekend. Don't you think?'

Simone nodded, standing to hug her Mum.

'It's going well so far, don't you think?'

'I do. Tracey and I have clicked. It's like we've been friends for ages, which we have, in the virtual world, but, you know what I mean.'

Simone and Vicky laughed.

'We do,' said Vicky, reaching out to take Simone's hand. 'I feel the same way, and I think Simone does too.'

Simone squeezed Vicky's hand.

'I do.'

'How about you, Jackie? Feeling out of your depth or are you keeping afloat?' asked Maggie.

Jackie took a moment to consider.

'This is so hot. I'm as randy as hell and I cannot wait to see what's going to happen next.'

Everyone laughed.

'In fact,' said Jackie, standing.

Maggie, Simone, and Vicky watched as Jackie removed her clothes, throwing each garment onto the bed until she was fully nude.

Ta da,' she said, arms out wide.

The other girls clapped.

'Well done,' said Maggie. 'Your Mum's not there yet but I suspect she will get there.'

Jackie nodded.

'I think so too. She took an age sorting through her underwear earlier this week and I think she may have even bought a new set. Though,' Jackie added looking down at her nudity. 'they may be rather redundant.'

The girls laughed again.

'Oh, I don't know,' said Maggie. 'Perhaps baby steps are in order. Liane might feel more comfortable stripping down to her underwear. That way she's not fully dressed nor fully nude.'

'Great idea,' said Jackie. 'What me to suggest it?'

Maggie thought before nodding.

'Yes. Once she sees you're naked, she's bound to say something to you. Use that opportunity to suggest she show off her new lingerie.'

Jackie nodded.

'I'd better get down there. Enjoy yourselves ladies but not too much.'

'Yes, Mum.'

After Maggie left.

'What did she mean, not too much?' asked Jackie.

'We're building a poly family,' said Simone. 'And agreed we'd share everything initially. No pairing off, things like that. It more applies to Mum,' Simone laughed. 'Mum number two, I guess and Philip.'

'The concern was Philip would connect with Maggie as they live so close, leaving Tracey out. So we agreed we'd do everything together.'

Jackie laughed.

'Were they worried about one of you two hooking up with Philip?'

Simone and Vicky looked at each other before turning their attention back to Jackie.

'Yep.'

'It's not as outrageous as you look,' said Simone, laughing. 'He's a lot older but not out of the question.'

'Simone!' exclaimed Jackie. 'He's old enough to be your Dad, no, your Granddad.'

Vicky laughed.

'My dad was much older than my Mum when they got married. Much older. It's not unusual given our lifestyle desires and choices.'

'Fair enough. What is next? Do you know?' asked Jackie.

'Mum wants to feel the bite of the cane,' said Simone

'The cane, really?' said Jackie, wide eyed. 'That's going to hurt.'

'We hope so.'

'You too?' asked Jackie.

Simone nodded.

'I'm only getting six, Mum's getting twelve.'

'On that bench?' asked Jackie.

'Yep. You'll get a great view of my Mum's bits and pieces.'

'And yours,' said Vicky.

Simone blushed.

'Oh right, I'd forgotten about that. You too have dallied a little already,' said Vicky. 'So Jackie's already familiar.'

'You told?' said Jackie.

Maggie shrugged.

'Sure. Vicky is my poly sister. We don't have secrets. Besides, I didn't know it was a secret.'

'Well, it wasn't a secret as such, I told my Mum,' said Jackie.

'You told your Mum!' exclaimed Simone.

Vicky laughed.

'No secrets, remember.'

Simone laughed.

'What's good for the goose.'

'Exactly.'

Vicky and Simone hugged.

'I can't join your poly family, as I have a family but can I be a sister?' said Jackie.

'Course, silly,' said Vicky and Simone, opening up their hug, bringing Jackie into their fold and hugging her close. 'Why do you think you and your Mum were invited to this weekend in particular? We're hoping you'll be their first of our special friends.'

'Oh I think that's for sure,' said Jackie. 'We're no strangers to discipline as you know. This.... this is a little more kinky mind. But I like it, we like it,' said Jackie.

'You can speak for your Mum?' asked Simone.

'Yes, I think we know each other well enough for me to be confident about that. Mum's not going to want to walk away from this. Not now the door has been opened. How far she will walk through it, time will tell but me, I'm all in.'

'Have you ever been with a girl before?' asked Simone.

Jackie shook her head.

'That will be part of it.'

Jackie nodded.

'Now?'

Simone and Vicky shook their heads.

'No, we're sharing, remember. We'll all get sticky together,' said Vicky.

'Sticky?' laughed Simone.

'Hot, sweaty, wet, very, very, wet,' said Vicky. 'Sticky is a good word, don't you think?'

'I prefer sweaty,' said Jackie.

'Can't we go with sexy?' asked Simone. 'As in, we'll get sexy together.'

'I like it,' said Vicky.

'Me too,' said Jackie.

'GIRLS!'

'Show time,' said Simone.

Vicky took her hand. Jackie the other.

'Ready?' asked Vicky.

'As I'll ever be,' said Simone.

'Is it bad I'm so turned on right now,' whispered Jackie as they went downstairs.

'No, I'm so wet it's embarrassing,' said Simone. 'And I'm the one about to show the world just how much.'

'The world?' laughed Vicky. 'Exaggerate much.'

The girls' laughter drew smiles from the Mothers and Philip as they walked into the lounge. Maggie already straddling a bench.

Simone couldn't resist and nipped round the back, or the front depending on one's perspective, her hand covering her mouth as she saw just how much was on show.

'Oh my.'

'Not helping,' said Maggie.

Everyone laughed.

Jackie took her seat next to Liane who whispered something. Jackie whispered back. Liane smiled, nodded and excused herself.

'No, Mum, do it here.'

Liane stopped midway between her seat and the door.

'Do what?' asked Philip.

'Mum's going to strip down to her undies,' said Jackie, committing her mother in case she tried to back out.

'We would prefer it if you shared with us,' said Philip.

Liane nodded, her hands immediately reaching behind her.

'Let me help,' said Vicky, her deft fingers undoing the row of buttons down the back of Liane's dress in a flash.

'Thanks,' said Liane, smiling, despite her hot red cheeks, as she let the dress slide down her body before stepping out.

'I'll hang it up,' said Tracey, picking it up and disappearing out of the room.

'Nice undies, Mrs Granger.'

'Liane, please,' said Liane. 'I think we are passed the formalities wouldn't you say.'

Vicky chuckled.

'I would, yes.... Liane.'

Liane nodded and took her seat, somewhat eagerly, though whether that was because of her partial nudity or desire not to miss anything she never said.

'Simone,' said Philip, flexing the cane between his hands.

Simone nodded and straddled the bench before leaning forward.

'Are you going to give them a warm up spanking?' asked Liane.

'Would you like too?' asked Philip.

'Me?' squeaked Tracey.

'If you want too?'

'I would love too.'

Simone gave a low moan.

'Are you ok?' asked Liane.

'It's a fantasy of hers,' said Tracey, as she walked back into the room. 'To be spanked by a woman other than me.'

'I'd love to spank her,' said Liane

Simone smiled shyly.

'You're smiling now,' said Jackie.

The mothers laughed, including Maggie, though she was acutely aware of her openly exposed position.

'Talking of warm ups, I never got a warm up when caned at school,' said Liane. 'Maggie wants to experience what I had.'

'You were caned at school?'

Liane nodded.

'It was delicious. Hurt to blazes mind. First time, I got four. Then it was six from then on, the last time it was ten. I can tell you I was a bag of nerves waiting to enter the Headmistresses office for that one.'

'Sounds like you were caned a lot,' said Jackie.

'Can we discuss this later?' asked Simone. 'I'm kind of exposed here.'

'Hush,' said Liane. 'Yes, like Maggie here, once I hit puberty spanking became a large part of my life. I craved it as much as I feared it. No, fear is not the right word. I cannot think of one right now, but I will. Anyway, I would get caned at school, and then have to give my Mum a punishment slip which meant I got spanked at home. Hand then hairbrush. Man, that thing hurt.'

'More than the cane?'

'Good question. They hurt in different ways. The cane bites. The pain stinging hot on the surface and then slowly sinks down into the bottom. The hairbrush thuds more, the pain deeper immediately. The cane leaves welts, the hairbrush bruises.'

'The hairbrush on top of cane welts must have been an experience.'

'I hadn't really thought about it as that was the usual for me. But yes, the hairbrush re-ignited the stinging lines of the welts.'

'So are Maggie and Simone going to get a hairbrush spanking after they are caned?' asked Jackie.

'Jackie! Don't give him ideas,' said Simone.

'Great idea,' said Philip. 'It will be truly authentic then.'

Simone groaned.

'Ignore her,' said Jackie. 'She practically just wet herself back here.'

'Jackie!'

SLAP

Jackie sat back, smiling.

'Hush, grown-ups talking.'

'Were you spanked at school?' asked Liane

142

'Yes,' said Tracey.

'You were?' asked Vicky surprised. 'What happened to no secrets?'

'That's for now, not the past,' said Tracey. 'I went to boarding school, so spanking was rife. Teachers spanked in the classroom, Dorm Prefects spanked in the Dorms, Prefects spank in the hallways, so embarrassing, and the Headmistress of course.'

'Caned?'

'Only the Head. Teachers tended to use the Tawse, it's a leather strap. Prefects, the hairbrush.'

'On the bare?' asked Simone.

'Yes, always.'

'Really?' asked Liane. 'The Head always threatened pulling my knickers down but never did. Mum, though, always.'

'We always got a hand spanking warm up though. Makes me wonder just how much was punishment and how much was pleasure for them.'

'Oh, I have no doubt my Headmistress enjoyed caning me. I was there too many times for her to really think I was a delinquent, that and my grades. Straight A student.'

'Now that she has shared,' said Jackie, with a groan. 'Soooo many times.'

Laughter.

'Ok, let's cane Maggie cold,' said Philip. 'And Liane, perhaps you would like to add a few more smacks to that lovely hand print you have left behind on Simone's bottom.'

'Me?'

'Sure. Simone will be mortified of course, and that's without going over Jackie's knee later. That will be so much more mortifying.'

Simone groaned.

'Hush,' said Jackie, bringing her hand down across Simone's bottom, evening up the other cheeks.

'Ow!' said Simone.

Jackie delivered a sound hand spanking, alternating cheeks as she went.

'You're doing a good job there,' said Philip.

'Long time spankee, first time spanker,' said Jackie, her hand falling hard and fast. 'I think that will do.'

Jackie stood back, looking intently between Simone's thighs.

'Lovely and wet too.'

Simone just moaned.

'Really, let me look,' said Philip.

Simone groaned again and covered her head with her arms.

'Soaking wet,' agreed Philip. 'Her vagina is opening nicely and her clit is actually throbbing.'

'I noticed that,' said Jackie. 'Mom can spank Simone first, and then cane Maggie next,' she suggested. 'Let Simone dwell a little on her wet pussy. Trust me, she can feel the wetness as it trickles down and she knows from watching Vicky's spanking she'll be dripping too.'

'I'm making a note of all this,' said Simone.

'I bet you are,' said Jackie, gently poking Simone's cheek.

'Ok, I propose on giving six to Maggie, then six to Simone before completing Maggie's punishment.'

'Ohhh, nice,' said Liane. 'The pain of the stripes will be sinking in whilst knowing she has another six on top of those to come. Ten in one go left little time to think about what was happening. I like it. I see what you mean.'

'Told you,' said Maggie.

Philip tapped the cane across Maggie's cheeks.

'Ready?'

'Yes, Sir.'

The cane landed with a SNAP!

Maggie cried out.

'One,' said Vicky, moving to kneel in front of Maggie, taking her hands in hers.

SNAP!

'Two.'

Maggie was panting after six of the best and initially glad of the respite as she listened to Simone's cries and the snap of the cane across her bottom. But as her own bottom throbbed with the pain of her first six, she began to think about the six she still had to come. Her tummy flipped and she even wondered whether she could take them.

'Ok, Six more.'

Maggie lifted her head but if she was going to say something it was lost in her yelp as the bite of the cane bit cruelly, the welt crossing those already laid down.

'One,' said Liane, having replaced Jackie, holding Maggie's hand.

After the fourth.

'Headmistress would always make the last two bite harder,' Liane said.

Maggie looked at Liane, who winked. Maggie cried out.

'That's five. One more. Across the back of her thighs. Headmistress would save that spot for the really naughty girls.'

SNAP!

Maggie screamed.

'Lovely,' said Liane, placing her hands either side of Maggie's face and kissing her soundly. 'Ok?'

Maggie nodded.

'Hurts like the blazes but yeah, lovely.'

Many hands helped Maggie to stand, instantly hugged by Simone.

'You ok?'

Simone nodded.

'Lovely.'

'You.'

'Yep.'

'Time for lunch,' said Philip. 'Liane, Vicky, please do the honours. Jackie, perhaps you could give them a hand.'

'Sure,' said Jackie, jumping up. 'Happy too.'

Philip smiled as Jackie's boobs jiggled as she stood and ran out after the others, seemingly comfortable with her nudity. He looked about.

This is perfect, he thought, looking at the naked women standing in the room, the three that just left and a very handsome woman wearing sexy lingerie that heighted her sexuality and provided a delicious counterpoint to the other girls' nudity.

Having at least one woman dressed, even only partially is the way to go, he thought, noticing the blush on Simone's face as she looked at Tracey, her brain reminding her she was fully nude once more.

Humiliation: The Beginnings Book Two.
CHAPTER SIX
BEFORE I MET MY MASTER

My submissive journey started way before I met my Master, way before I even knew my desires and need would lead me to a life of deepest subservience. No, it started, I guess, as many of us do, with a few swats from a boyfriend in the lead up to sex, then, once I connected my thoughts, like joining the dots of a puzzle without knowing the picture it would reveal, I realised I enjoyed spanking. I found myself actively seeking novels and erotic stories on line that contained spanking, masturbating to thoughts of being over the knee, getting my buns warmed and then venturing onto the net and the chat rooms, hearing from Dominants about their plans for my behind, which thrilled me greatly. Still, it took a while to go from the cerebral to the reality of a spanking. Which, again seems very common and perhaps I fall into the minority of actually persevering with the thoughts and fantasy to experiencing a spanking for real.

Actually, my first time was both everything I imagined and a little disappointing at the same time. The build up was great, the anticipation and trepidation in equal measure warred within me, both stoking up my arousal, keeping it bubbling, keeping me wet, that's for sure, and the afternoon was everything I asked for. Light, nothing to heavy, with plenty of spanking, both from his hand and paddle. The disappointment came later, as I lay in bed, fingers idly stroking my pussy realising my bottom bore no reminders of my afternoon. The sting had quickly faded. By the time I got home there was no redness and certainly no bruising.

I shared this with my Dom and we arranged a second visit where the spanking was certainly more intense. But I still felt something was missing.

After a few months of regular visits and nicely warmed arse each time, my research ventured into Discipline and spankings and other punishments as a consequence of some action or misbehaviour. I quickly joined the dots, having had some experience under my (or perhaps that phrase for us subs should be... beneath his...) belt, it didn't take me long for a new picture to emerge.

One that took me on a journey I hadn't expected.

For context, I am tiny, just about 5feet tall, I am slender, 34a cup size often taken to be a young teenager than my true age (ok, maybe not so much now, but certainly at the time of my experiences with Domestic Discipline). I still have a nose around the children's section in clothes shops, as I love a bargain, they have some pretty cool stuff and they still fit me!

*

I was hot and tired. The flight from the UK was soooo long and involved several changes to get down to the southern states where the couple I was planning on spending the summer lived.

After discovering Discipline as perhaps more the lifestyle element I had been missing, I had spent the preceding months searching for disciplinarians, but whilst I was being spanked for breaking certain rules, the experience was still lacking.....something.

Then I got talking to John and Jackie. A married couple living "down South" in the good old U S of A. They were in their forties, living in a small rural community where discipline was the norm for every household, many wives also experiencing being Taken In Hand (which for those not used to the terminology means, the submissive within a Domestic Disciplined relationship, or even more basic, punished for rule breaking and so on) and certainly the daughters within their households. The boys were a different matter, once reaching their teen years, they would more often be seen toiling the land, so to speak, with labour intensive chores, only rarely would a teen boy be "taken to the woodshed."

The more they spoke of the life of the women within the community the more I gravitated to the Domestic Disciplined way of life. Something just clicked. The spanking was one thing, the physical thing, but having real consequences to my actions, having the truly important decisions in my life made for me, though still having a voice and being heard, was appealing. To just be me, knowing my excesses and exuberances would be lovely but strictly dealt with, joined the dots to a picture that was perfect for me.

We chatting constantly, sometimes the information overload pushed me back a little, but I always returned, having digested the contents of the mails they sent, the pictures, the books they encouraged me to read, my mind buoyed by the possibilities the lifestyle offered. The fear was still there of course. We are talking about me moving to the States for three months as a trial, staying on longer if all parties desired and it was scary. I would be leaving my friends and family behind. My job, I didn't care about that. I knew, upon return, I could simply pick up where I left of, and in my heart I knew my friends and family would still be there, and John and Jackie were most insistent that I keep in regular contact with them, including a video call at least once a week with my folks. Rules were discussed and agreed, consequences also, and the one aspect hitherto unmentioned, sex.

When Jackie brought this up during a one to one video conference we were having, she was asking about my thoughts on having sex with John. How was I to respond? John was Jackie's husband and my mind was questioning whether this was a test to see if I had unwanted designs on her husband. Maybe this showed upon my face or my hesitancy prompted Jackie to offer up more information about their thoughts, I don't know, I am just glad she did. Jackie assured me that their hopes were that I would freely engage in sexual activities with them. (The use of the word "them" sent my mind whirling as I considered myself straight, never having been with a girl before - which, before you start yelling at the pages, I know flies in the face of my experience with Heather and Judy, but honestly, I didn't even think about that as a lesbian experience, or think about it much at all really. It had been just one of those things girls did.

This was different. This was conscious, premeditated and distinctly sexual interaction with another girl, woman actually as she more than twice my age, just (I was just turning 21 at this point). I found myself nodding my head in agreement despite the whirlwind of emotions in my head, especially as Jackie had gone on to say there would be others too. Other men and women who they met socially and sexually that I would be interacting with both disciplinarily and sexually.

Every way I looked at is, I was jumping in with both feet. All my thoughts and fantasies becoming reality in one big melting pot, and my pussy tingled happily whilst my head warred with doubts and fears, longing and need.

So here I am, waving at John and Jackie as they stand, holding a board with my name on it, waving back, smiles beaming.

I couldn't say I had thought in detail about those first moments, nor the next couple of hours but if I had, I doubt I would have come up with anything remotely like what actually happened.
We greeted each other with warm hugs and kisses and then Jackie held be at arm's length, wrinkling up her nose.

You're all hot and sweaty,' Jackie said.

'Yeah, long flight, long flights actually,' I said.

'It's yes, dear, not yeah,' corrected Jackie. 'Let's get you out of those smelly clothes and into something nice and fresh shall we. John, be a dear and bring the car around, we won't be long.'

With that, I was spun around by the shoulders and with a gentle pressure between my shoulders steered towards the bathrooms.

'Excellent, we can use this one,' said Jackie.

It took me a moment to see the sign for "Baby Changing" on the wall besides the door.

My tummy fluttered a little but no alarm bells were ringing just yet. The room was after all more comfortable for two and private.
That's when my tummy flipped. It was not quite as private as I was used too, when using the bathroom.

'Slip out of those clothes first,' said Jackie, 'then you must be busting for a pee.'

Her words brought my attention to my protesting bladder, suddenly more insistent then the gentle pressure of only seconds ago, and I practically ripped my clothes off before rushing to the toilet in the corner.

'Wait one second, missy,' said Jackie. 'Panties and bra first.'

I didn't stop to think, I just pulled the top over my head and pushed my panties down my ankles, throwing the bra into her waiting hands and kicking the panties up into the air, both to free them from my ankles and hand them over in one deft move.

Jackie chuckled as she snatched them from the air.

'Nice,' she said. 'You'll have to try out for the soccer team.'

I sat myself down and willed myself to relax, but nothing was happening.

'Everything ok, dear?'

'I, urrrrrm, could I have some privacy?' I asked, feeling my face heat up.

'Privacy, dear, what could be more private than this?'

Worst than showing no intention of leaving the small room, Jackie was actually approaching. Even worse, she was kneeling down. Oh my god, her hands are on my knees and the subtle pressure to part them was clear. The frown on her face more so as I resisted.

'Open,' Jackie commanded in a voice that brooked no argument.

My mouth opened nevertheless then snapped shut as I looked into her eyes and saw steely determination and her lips which twitched with a suppressed smile.

All those chats about disobedience and the consequences came tumbling through my mind and my knees parted, and kept going as Jackie's hands gently eased them open.

Christ, what is she planning to do stick her head up there, I thought as my muscles twinged in protest as my thighs were parted to their limit.

I almost laughed aloud when Jackie took my dismay wrongly.

'Don't worry, dear, we'll work on your flexibility, you'll be doing the splits in no time.'

The splits!

I was looking directly at Jackie as she stared intently at my privates so I saw the frown deepen.

'You're not shaved?'

I shook my head, realising we had never discussed this aspect of my grooming. My bush was my pride and joy. The one and only thing I could point to, to say, Hey! Look! I'm not a kid! Not that I ever whipped it out whilst being carded at the pubs and clubs I frequented, but it was nice having it whilst changing at the gym for instance, or at the Doctors for my downstairs check-ups.

'No,' I said. More to fill the silence I think. 'Is that a problem?'

Jackie sat back, clearly mulling things over.

'No, not a problem, we can fix that soon enough.'

The change in conversation from me peeing to my pubic hair was enough for my muscles to relax and my stream to flow.

Flow, how quaint.

It thundered.

Literally, it was such a torrent it hit the water below with a noise I can only relate to when a horse pees. Ever seen and heard that? Well, imagine that and then take it up a couple of notches as the small, white tiled room amplified the sound. I placed my hands in my head as Jackie chuckled. Any attempt to snap my knees together thwarted, as Jackie, whilst having stood to consider the o'naturel state of my bush, stayed closed enough that her legs blocked my knees. The slight tug of a smile now prominent as she caught my eye.

My tummy flipped and fluttered and my pussy tingled, and my nipples lengthened.

Ok, I had better get this bit out of the way, as it does play a part, well several parts within my recollections to come. Whilst I have small breasts, small even for my frame, my nipples are huge, not just in comparison, but huge. Easily half an inch, over when really turned on and sooooo sensitive, the slightest touch sends my pussy into sexual overdrive and readiness, turning on the taps of my liquid arousal to the point of dripping. Soooooo embarrassing.

Finally, the torrent petered out and I reached for the tissue only for my hand to be smacked away and, mortified, I watched as Jackie peeled off a couple of sheets and deftly, though a little longer than I usually would, wiped my pussy dry. As I went to rise, face burning, she placed her hand on my shoulder, sitting me back down. Confused, I watched her open her handbag, pull out a plastic packet, pluck out a wet wipe and proceeded to wipe my pussy again, with firmer strokes and with more determination to ensure every millimetre was attended too.

'Ok, let's get you dressed.'

That's when I realised John has taken my bags to the car.

'I don't have anything else with me,' I said.

'Not to worry,' said Jackie. 'I brought something, just in case.'
Jackie was back into her bag, pulling out several items before handing me a pair of panties.

I looked at them, then at Jackie in disbelief.

They were white with little pink flowers on. Cute, for a child, not something a grown woman would wear.

The thought occurred first, then the realisation of the conversations with John and Jackie and their continued reminder that I would be treated as their niece, with strict rules more in keeping with a teenager than a grown, independent woman.

I had been so caught up the eroticism of my thoughts, my imagination and my interpretation of what it all meant; I'd never stop to consider there might be another version.   A John and Jackie version.

My fears were confirmed with her next sentence.

'You won't be needing a bra, you haven't got much anyway and just vests and camisoles are more in keeping with a thirteen year old niece.'

'Th, Th, Th, Thirteen?' I stammered

'Yes, dear. It's what we've been talking about all this time.'

I cast my memory back over the many, many conversations we had had but was certain there had never been a mention of an age, especially not one as young as thirteen.

'Here,' said Jackie.

I looked directly at Jackie and could see the amused look on her face. Then I looked at the dress and groaned.

'Seriously,' I said, holding it up.

'You don't have to wear it,' Jackie said. 'Go as you are if you like.
Though we will have a conversation about that when we get home.'

I looked for my old clothes but realised they had disappeared into Jackie's bag no doubt. With little choice I stepped into the bright yellow dress and pulled it up, wriggling my hips to help it work its way up.

Jackie turned me around and helped the dress up over my shoulders before zipping it up. It was a snug fit and my boobs were pressed even flatter.

'Perfect,' said Jackie. 'I have socks and sandals here, and then we can go. John will start to wonder what we're up to in here.'

I pulled on the socks, leaving them around the ankles, and slipped my feet into the black shoes with gold buckles on the side. Jackie knelt and pulled the socks all the way up to just below my knees.

'Don't you look cute,' she said, turning me to face the mirror.

The girl looking back was every bit thirteen years old, wearing clothing a ten year old wouldn't be seen dead in, though the yellow did go well with my black hair.

With a firm smack on my bottom, I was propelled towards the door which I quickly opened and skipped ahead, narrowly missing a second swipe. I laughed, turning my head to poke my tongue out at Jackie, before skipping away.
Jackie laughed too and followed behind.

It wasn't until I left the airport, stopping to look for John that I realised *I'd skipped!*

Jackie's arm around me, hand on my shoulder steered me towards an estate car, a station wagon I recall they are called in the States, and slipped on to the back seat.

'Slight detour, John,' said Jackie. 'We're going to Laura's salon.'

'Is she expecting us?' asked John.

'I'll call her on the way.'

I wasn't taking much notice of this; I was too busy trying to pull the hem of the dress down a little bit as it was so short, it barely covered my panties.

John looked over his shoulder and down so obviously my face burned hotly.

'Cute panties,' he said with a chuckle before turning his attention forwards and starting the car. Jackie was already on her cell.

Humiliation: The Beginnings Book Two.
FAMILY SPANKING

'All right, girls. If my spankings are no longer making an impression then perhaps a spanking from my boyfriend will.

Simon looked up surprised as Fiona walked in pushing Alison and Wendy before her.

Mom! You're not serious,' moaned Alison.

'Deadly. Your behaviour is getting out of hand.'

'We said we were sorry,' said Wendy.

'Saying sorry to me is not going to save you both from a damned good spanking, young lady. And then you're going to say sorry to the Mom who complained about you both on Facebook. FACEBOOK! I could have died when I read that.'

'They didn't mention us by name, Mom. No one needs to know,' said Alison.

'I know,' said Fiona, 'and so will that Mom as soon as I am done with you.'

'I cannot believe you told the world you were going to spank us,' moaned Alison.

'Stop your moaning,' said Fiona. 'I simply said you would get an old fashioned punishment and, as you say, no one on Facebook knows it was you messing around in that theatre.'

'But, if we have to go and apologise, she will know.'

'Thank yourself lucky I'm not spanking you both in front of her,' said Fiona. 'I considered that, you know.'

Both girls looked at each other.

'Now, Simon. I want you to punish both these girls, you hear. Spank them so they cannot sit down for a week. A punishment they will not forget, ever.'

Simon looked at Fiona then at the girls.

'If you're sure.'

'I am.'

'Girls, jeans and panties off, then choose a corner and stand in it. Noses to the wall. I'll call you once I have decided your punishments and gathered the necessary implements.'

'Oh,' said Fiona. 'No, I wasn't thinking of embarrassing them so much. Just pull their panties down once they're over your knee.'

Simon looked to the girls.

'I gave you both an instructions. Last warning. Fiona, if you want me to punish them I will. Or you can do it. But I cannot have you undermining me every step of the way.'

'No, no, you're right,' said Fiona. 'I want you to punish them. My spankings are proving ineffectual.'

'You need to add a level of embarrassment,' said Simon. 'It adds to the intensity of the spanking and defiantly the part of their punishment they will remember.'

Fiona nodded.

Simon turned to the girls.

'You had your warning. Now you have earned yourself additional punishments for your disobedience. I suggest you do as you're told before things get really serious for you both.'

Alison and Wendy looked to their Mom who looked from her girls to Simon, opened her mouth then closed it again before saying,

'You heard him, girls. Do you you're told.'

Both girls exchanged looks, their faces red as their fingers fumbled with their jeans, undoing the buttons before pushing them and their panties down their thighs, clearing their bottoms at the back but keeping their panties high enough to cover their front.

Simon held Alison's gaze without saying a word.

'Fine.'

Alison pushed her jeans and panties down, scissoring her legs as she worked them off her feet to stand naked from the waist down.

Simon pointed to the corner.

Alison turned, walked to the corner, placing her nose to the wall.

'Wendy?'

'Please, Mom.'

'Simon.'

Simon turned to Fiona.

'Last warning for you too.'

Fiona blanched.

'Get 'em off, young lady,' she said.

Wendy pushed her jeans and panties down, and she too, was soon standing in the corner, nose to the wall.

Simon turned to Fiona.

'I planned to hand spank them both over my knee. Bend them over the arm of the sofa and strap them and finish up with your pussy paddle in the diaper position.'

'Simon!'

'Fiona, trust me, the girls know I spank you, they are not deaf.'

'Is that true, girls?'

Both girls nodded, red faced.

'Oh my gawd,' said Fiona, her hands covering her face.

Simon laughed.

'Look on the bright side,' he said. 'No more waiting until the middle of the night for your spankings.'

'Simon,' pleaded Fiona.

'I warned you the girls would eventually have to know. You know I wasn't happy trying to keep it a secret.'

'Yes, but...'

'No buts, Fiona.'

'Simon.' Fiona's tone had an edge.

'Enough,' said Simon. 'And lose that tone.'

Fiona closed her mouth, biting off her next word.

'Now, please go and fetch me your strap and pussy paddle.'

Fiona left the room.

*

Wendy began to kick her legs as Simon's spanking hand continued to lay down the first of her three punishments. Her bottom was a rosy red and she wailed and pleaded as his hand fell over and over.

'I think she's had enough,' said Fiona. 'Perhaps it's Alison's turn?'

Simon looked at Alison, who was standing, watching Wendy's spanking, hands on her head before returning her gaze to Fiona.

'Fiona. You had fair warning. Remove your clothes and stand by Alison, hands on your head.'

'What, wait!' said Fiona.

'No!' snapped Simon. 'You are making a mockery of the lifestyle arrangement we have worked so hard to create. I am the Head of House at your request. We have rules, we have an understanding, an understanding that includes punishment when you overstep, as you have done several times today already.'

'If you think I am going to stand naked, alongside my girls, you have another thing coming.'

'I think, Fiona. You are going to do just that *and* you are going to receive the same punishments as the girls, alongside the girls. You will share their fate for your behaviour.'

'Or what?'

'Or I leave.'

'Leave?'

'Yes. I made it very clear the lifestyle I am seeking and I am not going to compromise on that now. Especially having had a taste of what it can be like with you. It's been better then I imagined. Better then I fantasised and if I cannot have that with you, then I will resume my search once more.'

'I'm not saying I want to end our relationship,' said Fiona. 'I'm just setting some boundaries.'

'And they are unacceptable to me,' said Simon. 'I made that clear from our very first conversation.'

'It's true,' said Alison.

'Alison.'

'So your girls read our email correspondence.'

Fiona nodded.

'I told you I had no secrets from the girls.'

'You did. So why the late night spankings?'

'Too embarrassing, them hearing my spanking and stuff,' admitted Fiona. 'Them knowing about them was bad enough, but I didn't want any secrets or misunderstandings with the girls. You made a good point about that.'

Simon nodded.

'So earlier?'

Alison laughed.

'Mom never mentioned anything about a pussy paddle.'

'Your Mom lays on her back, holding her knees against her chest and apart, offering up her pussy and bottom to the paddle.'

'Simon!'

'The girls are going to both see and experience this for themselves, Fiona. Your time for privacy has expired. Your punishments going forward will be openly given.'

'I don't know I can do that, Simon.'

'You can, Mom,' said Wendy, lifting her head, still over Simon's lap. 'You've never been happier. You have to admit that.'

'It's true, Mom. We've both seen the change in you since you met Simon and started this lifestyle.'

Fiona looked from Alison to Wendy before throwing up her hands.

'It's true,' she said. 'Oh well.'

Fiona undid the buttons of her jeans.

Simon brought his hand down firmly across Wendy's rosy cheeks, resuming his spanking. Wendy cried out, her legs kicking within seconds.

Fiona pushed her pants and panties off her feet before placing her hands on her head.

'I said naked, Fiona. Take it all off.'

'But the girls....'

'You have a point. Alison, remove the rest of your clothing.'

'Mom!'

'What did I do?' said Mom, pulling her top up and over her head.

Alison pulled off her T-shirt, her bare breasts wobbling before they settled.

Mom was soon just as nude, and both girls stood hands on their heads.

'Ok, Wendy, join your Mom after removing the rest of your clothing.'

Wendy rose, giving her bottom a vigorous rub before removing her top and bra. Their mom's need of the lifestyle having allowed them to face their own punishments with a certain positivity.

The crisp sound of hand on flesh filled the room once more as Simon spanked Alison every bit as firmly as he had Wendy. Alison's white cheeks, turning pink, then red within minutes.

Knowing her turn was next had Fiona's tummy fluttering and her face burning as she faced the prospect of a spanking in front of her girls for the first time.

Funny though, she thought. *It doesn't feel as end of the world as I thought it would, In fact, there is a certain connection with my girls that hadn't been there before. An experience they were about to share.*

'Fiona.'

Alison stood next to Wendy, shifting her weight from one foot to the other as her bottom burned.

Fiona lay herself over Simon's lap, giving one glance to her girls, both standing hands over head, watching her before burying her face into the sofa and offering up her bottom for punishment.

'The family that spanks together, stays together,' said Simon, bringing his hand down with a resounding SLAP.

*

Fiona stuffed the corner of the pillow into her mouth to stifle her cries. Through her years of marriage she had always considered her sex life to have been a good one. Seldom faking her orgasms she enjoyed sex and had no complaints. Since meeting Simon, her sex life had soared to new heights. She knew the lifestyle she and Simon had engaged in had a lot to do with the intensity of her orgasms and the frequency of multiple orgasms but she also had to give credit to Simon for his creativity and inventiveness when it came to sex. Exploring and tapping into deep reservoirs of sexual arousal from areas hitherto unexplored such as having her bottom spanked, pussy spanked, breast slapped, even having her face slapped, in the right context had proven incredibly arousing. Stuff she would have never thought of, like having Simon spit into her open mouth, forced to taste herself, drink his pee, drink her own pee! Activities not even viewed on pornhub she now found part of her thoughts, fantasises and everyday sex life. One new element she could not deny as she screamed her third orgasm in as many minutes into the pillow was humiliation. The images of her girls watching as she spread her legs wide, exposing her pussy for the paddle burned her with shame and embarrassment that tightened her core and drove her arousal to heady heights that had her light headed as a fourth began to build.

'No, no, no, no more,' she gasped. 'Please.'

Simon sat back grinning.

'As you said please.'

Fiona collapsed on to the bed, her bottom and pussy still smarting from their spankings, her muscles already aching from the repetitive contractions forced through her orgasms. As they lay on the bed, a soft cry filtered through into their bedroom and they looked at each other before laughing quietly.

'Seems you are not the only one in need of sexual release after your punishment.'

'I guess not.'

They listened intently.

'Can you hear that?' asked Fiona.

'No, what?'

'I swear I can hear a vibrator.'

'One of them hasn't quite finished yet,' said Simon.

'What should we do?'

'Do?'

'Well, I can't just lay here listening to one of my girls masturbating.'

'Want to go and watch?' asked Simon.

'No!' said Fiona slapping Simon's arm. 'Bet you would. Perve.'

Simon laughed.

'How about I open our door and spank you again.'

Simon's dick stirred despite its recent exertions as he saw the spark of arousal within Fiona's eyes.

Fiona groaned and cupped her sex.

'Ohh don't,' she complained. 'You've killed my pussy.'

Simon laughed.

'Still hear it?'

Fiona went silent for a moment before shaking her head.

'See, just needed a distraction.'

Fiona lifting herself off the bed just enough to kiss Simon full on the lips before collapsing back.

*

'Mom, seriously, close your door when you're having sex,' complained Alison.

'I do,' protested Fiona.

Wendy laughed.

'Then use a pillow or something, all your squeals and moans is a little off putting when I'm trying to concentrate.'

Fiona went bright red.

'I was,' she admitted, before laughing.

Both her girls burst out laughing.

Fiona felt closer to her girls than ever before.

'Which one of you was using the vibrator?'

Wendy put her hand up, blushing hotly.

'You heard?'

'Just, faintly. Simon couldn't hear it but I could.'

'Thank gawd for that,' said Wendy.

'That means it was you both Simon and I heard,' said Fiona, looking at Alison over the rim of her coffee.

'Nooooooo,' said Alison. You're making that up. I was being so quiet.'

'So I thought was I,' said Fiona, laughing.

'You are pretty loud,' said Wendy.

'You too?'

Wendy nodded.

'Oo, Oooo, Ooooo, oOOOOOOO,' mimicked Wendy before laughing.

Fiona and Alison laughed, though Alison took a playful swipe at Wendy.

'None of that,' said Fiona. 'Or I'll send you both to see Simon.'

Both girls looked at each other before looking back at Fiona.

'Promises, promises,' said Wendy.

Fiona laughed.

'Did you know Simon ask me how I felt about spanking you,' said Alison, looking at Fiona.

'You, spank me!' exclaimed Fiona. 'I hope you said no.'

'Why would I say that?' asked Alison.

'You never did,' said Fiona.

Alison nodded.

'Apparently humiliation is a big turn on for you.'

Fiona only paused for a moment before nodding.

'And we know spanking has a mentally positive effect so what's to decide.'

'I'll die of embarrassment.'

'That's the idea, though you'll not actually die, but I'll settle for you wanting the ground to open up and swallow you whole.'

Fiona's tummy flipped.

'When did he asked you?'

'This morning. Though I reckon we've all got a few days grace if you bottom is a bruised as mine.'

Wendy nodded.

'My cheeks protest every time I sit down.'

'Mine too,' said Fiona. 'Kind of nice.'

Both Wendy and Fiona nodded.

'Talking of embarrassment,' said Fiona, 'Did you know Simon reached out to the Mom who complained?'

Wendy nodded.

'He said he'd connected with her last night on Facebook.'

'Did he mention during that conversation he told her of your punishment.'

'Noooo,' said Alison. 'It's going to be so much harder facing her now, knowing that.'

Fiona laughed, looking down into her mug as she said, 'Simon's suggested the Mom spank you both.'

Twin, 'Noooooooooo's,' filled the air.

*

'So, how do you feel about me spanking you after yesterday?' asked Alison.

'Pretty good, actually,' said Fiona. 'At first, I thought Simon was going to get you to give me a random spanking, which bothered me more because that's more sexual than discipline. But given that I yelled at you in front of your friends and for something you didn't actually do. I deserved the spanking and from you, so yes, I feel pretty good about it. You?'

'Honestly?'

Fiona nodded.

'Please.'

'I loved it.'

'Alison!'

'What, I did. I never thought I would but I really did. Is that bad?'

Fiona thought for a microsecond before shaking her head.

'I'd rather you enjoy it than feel bad about it.'

'And you got the humiliation you were seeking.'

'You asking?'

'Oh, No, that's a statement. You soaked my jeans.'

Fiona's mouth was just open in shock before she hid her face in her heads, much to the amusement of the girls who were already laughing.

'By my count you must have cum three times at least.'

'You could tell.'

'I could yes. I don't think Simon could. It's well disguised with all the kicking, wriggling and writhing we all do. If I hadn't climaxed over your knee at least a dozen times and every time over Simon's I probably wouldn't have known either.'

'You said you thought Simon was going to have Alison give you a random spanking? Does Simon do that?' asked Wendy.

'Sometimes,' said Fiona. 'We agreed, as Head of House, he could and should not only spank me when I break the rules but anytime he chooses.'

'I was reading up on this Domestic Discipline you two have got going but usually it's sex that the Head of House wants to be able to demand any time anywhere.'

'Oh we have that too. He took me over his counter not an hour ago.'

All three girls gazed at the counter contemplatively for about ten seconds.

'How do you feel about your visit to the Mom this afternoon?'

'You know, not as bad as I thought I would,' said Alison.

'Me, nether. I'm sort of resigned to my fate, if you know what I mean.'

'It feels right too,' said Alison. 'We both behaved appallingly and even though Simon thoroughly spanked us. Getting spanked by the mom we wronged will be the truly absolving factor.'

'I'm glad you feel that way,' said Fiona.

Alison nodded.

Wendy on the other hand, caught a look in Fiona's eye.

'Why?'

'Oh, well you know she wasn't alone at the theatre. She had her two boys with her. Well, they're getting to watch your spankings.'

Twin, 'Noooooooooo's,' filled the air.

*

Booze

'What in the world is all this?'

Caroline sprung to her feet, red wine flying from her glass to land across the occasional table and the white rug beneath.

Gasps echoed as each of the girls looked from the dripping wine to Caroline's mother in all her fury.

'Mom? I thought you were away until next week.'

'Obviously. And I thought we could trust you.'

'We.'

'Don't take that tone with me, young lady. Clifford is my boyfriend and you will show him some respect as long as you are under my roof.'

'You want me to leave.'

'Caroline,' said Clifford. 'You know that's not true. Why do you keep pushing that line?'

'You can shut up.'

'Caroline! That's it young lady. You were in a world of trouble with this little lot, but know you're really in for it. Get into that corner.'

Caroline looked to the corner then back to her Mom, folding her arms, shaking her head and standing her ground.

Mom rose to her full five foot height, eyes blazing.

'You really want to do this, young lady?'

'I'm not doing anything,' said Caroline.

Mom looked at the table.

'Legal age to drink is twenty-one. Any of you girls twenty-one?'

All the girls shook their heads.

'Didn't think so. And if you carry on as you are, you won't live to see your nineteenth birthday, that's for damned sure.'

'You're not spanking me,' said Caroline. 'Not in front of my friends.'

'We can go,' said Laura.

'No you can't,' said Mom. 'Not yet. I'll tell you when you can go.'

'So, not a spanking,' said Mom. 'Fine with me, grounding it is.'

'Three months,' said Clifford.

More gasps.

'That's Mary's pool party,' said Angela.

'And Mark's,' said Sharon.

'The beach party,' said Amy.

'It's the whole summer,' said Lisa.

Caroline looked to the girls and back to her Mom.

'It's just one summer. Three months,' said Caroline with a nod of her head.

Mom smiled.

'That was Clifford's suggest,' said Mom, looking over at Clifford. 'Pussy boy. I was thinking more like six months.'

Gasps.

'The winter prom.'

'Mrs Green. Caroline is Captain of the Cheerleaders, surely she can still do that?'

Mom nodded.

Sighs of relief from the girls.

'For home games only. And it's straight home afterwards. I'll be there to personally drive her home.'

'I can drive myself,' said Caroline.

'Not without a car you can't,' said Mom.

Gasps.

'How am I supposed to get to school?'

'Bus,' said Clifford.

Mom shook her head.

'I will take her. Every morning and pick her up every afternoon. I will walk her right to the door and be waiting there to collect her there too.'

'Oh my,' said Sharon.

'Caroline, seriously. Take the spanking,' said Amy.

'Yeah. It can't be worse than social suicide,' said Laura.

'I'll have to take my pants and panties off,' said Caroline.'

'So, we're all girls,' said Angela.

'He's not,' said Caroline, throwing a look at Clifford.

'Him. He's old enough to be your Dad,' said Laura. 'He doesn't count.'

'Grand dad more like,' said Lisa. 'He's seen plenty in his time I bet.'

'I'm not that old,' said Clifford. 'Grand dad indeed.'

Caroline looked at Mom.

'Bare bottomed?'

'Bare everything.'

'Pauline?' said Clifford.

'Would you have me any less?' asked Mom, looking at Clifford.

'No, that's true. But you are..... wiser. Caroline here is making a youthful indiscretion.'

'Pussy boy. Caroline here has pushed things too far, by a long way. I'm not letting this one go, Clifford. If she chooses to be spanked, she's getting it from me and you.'

'Me?'

'Yes. It's time she accepted you as part of the family and it's time for you to step up and fully take on the role as Head of the Household.'

'He's not spanking me,' said Caroline.

Mom shrugged.

'Three months grounding in exchange for each of our spankings. You can mix it up if you like. As always the choice if yours.'

Caroline looked from Clifford, to Mom to the girls.

'Whilst you decide. Girls, take out your cell phones.'

The girls looked at each other.

'Now, ladies!' barked Mom.

The girls, jumped, each reaching for their cells, holding them out so Mom can see.

'Take some photos of the table. Five should cover it. Make sure you get the rug, and those bottles over there. The empty ones. Is that cake on my floor!'

'I dropped it,' said Amy. 'I'm so sorry.'

'Take a photo.'

After several minutes of "clicks" the girls looked at Mom expectantly.

'Ok, ladies, like out Caroline here, you have a choice. You can accept the spanking Caroline as been offered or send those photos to your Mom's.

I'll be following them up with my own text message, rest assured.'

The girls looked at each other.

'If we accept the spanking?' asked Lisa.

'Then nothing about this....,' Mom waved her hand to encompass the table, the bottles of wine and spirits upon it, the empty and half full classes, the cigarettes and the food strewn over the surface and on the floor, 'will be mentioned by me or Clifford.'

 Lisa nodded.

'I'll take the spanking.'

Caroline turned to her.

'You do realise she means fully naked and spanked by him as well as her.'

'I do, and please stop talking. I'm in for the same spanking you are going to accept and I suspect you are ramping up the minutes every time you open your mouth.'

'Who says.......'

'I do,' said Lisa.

'Me too,' said Amy. 'I'll take the spanking, Mrs Green.'

'And me,' said Laura. 'Not another word Caroline or we will spank you too.'

Caroline's mouth just opened and closed before she closed her eyes and nodded, accepting her fate.

'Ladies, clear this mess up. Caroline, be a dear and go and fetch your hairbrush please. The one I use to spank you bottom with. You know the one.'

Caroline's face was bright red as she practically ran out the door, desperate to stop her Mom from saying more.

Mom and Clifford stood together as the girls made quick work of the room.

'Move the table please, over there will do. Amy, that chair, front and centre.'

Turning to Clifford.

'You are a soft hearted, kind man, Clifford. Caroline is a tough as me, tougher actually, so are these girls. All are spanked at home, so this is not new to any of them, so don't spare their blushes or backsides.'

'Understood. You know you came close to joining the girls.'

Pauline slid her arm around Clifford's waist.

'I deserve it for the disrespect alone,' she said. 'And I feel bad the way Caroline has been treating you. I should have done something about that months ago.'

Clifford nodded.

'I don't disagree. Tomorrow night then.'

'In front of both the girls.'

'Naturally.'

'Fully nude, over your knee, bending over and diaper.'

'You want all that?'

'I do. I want the girls to see I am fully submissive to you and show them what's in store for them both going forwards. That should put an end to the behaviour of late and we can set about building a family that enjoys being together.'

'Amen to that.'

'Don't wimp out. We're all girls. We've all got the same bits and pieces, so humiliating yeah, but I'll live. So will the girls tonight, so no looking at your feet. You hear me?'

'I do. And I love you.'

'What?'

'I said I love you.'

'Picked a fine time to say that for the first time.'

'Want me to take it back?'

Pauline laughed, hugging and kissing Clifford.

'Don't you dare. I love you too.'

'Awwwww, that's so sweet,' said Amy.

'Thank you, Amy,' said Mom.

'My Dad spanks my Mom openly too,' Amy added quietly.

Mom nodded.

'I know. It's what gave me the idea. You Mom says it's created a special bond between you both. I would like that with my girls.'

'Really, that's so cool. I'd always felt that, but knowing Mom does too....' Amy skipped off to join the other girls.

'I didn't know they were all spanked too,' said Caroline, handing Mom the hairbrush.

'I didn't think you did. I was talking to the other Mom's about your spankings and was surprised just how many still spanked their girls too. Pleasantly surprised I might add. The Moms have my permission to spank you as I have for their girls, so you can expect many more spanking in your immediate future if you don't buck your ideas up.'

Caroline nodded.

'I know I've been off the rails lately, and I'm sorry, honest. Sometimes though, it's as if I just cannot help myself.'

'Teenage hormones,' said Mom. 'We all had them. I've been remiss in not taking firmer action with you girls. But that all stops tonight.'

'Yes, Mom,' said Caroline.

'Clothes off, ladies,' said Mom, stepping out of Clifford's arms. 'Clifford, if you sit here you will have the perfect view, and you can see their faces in the mirror.'

Gasps filled the room.

The Humiliation of Graham
Chapter One
THE AGREEMENT

Graham stopped dead, his heart missing a beat.

'Is something amiss, my dear?' asked his wife, Christine.

'Well, ermm, yes, errr, can I speak with you?'

'Why, dear? Is all not as we discussed? As we agreed?'

Graham's mind struggled to interpret the conversation he had had with his wife to what was in front of him.

'No, no, this is not what we agreed.'

'Is it not?' asked Christine. 'Did you not ask me to take charge, to assume the role of your Mistress?'

'Yes.....' said Graham, his eyes darted from place to place, his face as hot as a furnace.

'I see,' said Christine. 'And you thought it would be as you desired it, a power exchange, I think you called it, of pain giving and receiving?'

Graham swallowed and nodded.

'But it got me thinking,' Christine continued. 'If I am the Mistress, shouldn't it be as I desire it, not you?'

'Of course, yes,' Graham said immediately. 'Oh, I see,' he added.

'I knew you would,' said Christine warmly. 'You are not slow on the uptake and have always been able to reconcile new information within your existing understanding quickly.'

Graham grinned.

'I am a clever boy,' he said.

'You are,' said Christine. 'The question is, are you, or perhaps I should phrase that, were you, serious about the power exchange thing? That you want me to be in charge, not the normal boring everyday stuff, like bills, spending, where we go on holiday and the like, but of you, for me to be in charge of you? To use you for my desires, I think you put it, was that right?'

Graham nodded.

'It was. .... it is. That's what I want.'

'And your desires are pain based, am I right. Not exactly discipline, you don't want rules or anything, you just want me to beat you, is that right?'

197

Graham turned the words over in his head. They were sort of right, though he shied away from the word "beat" for some reason. That word had connotations of abuse that he didn't like, but the principal was there. He thought the idea of pain, pain from being spanked, paddled, caned would perhaps, help him banish the stresses of his work, the strain of being strong all the time. He wanted to let it all go, just for a time, just once in a while, though, if he were really being honest with himself he knew he wanted it far more regular than once in a while and for more than just stress release.

'Yes,' he said. 'You know I don't like the word *beat* but it's as good a word as any to describe what I desire.'

'And I will give you that, my darling. Only on my terms, my way and yes, my rules. You may not want rules, but there will be some to govern your behaviour when submitting to me. Can you live with that?'

'I can. I was referring to rules beyond the power exchange, rules governing the every day, those would not work, but rules within, those I can accept.'

Christine studied Graham, reading the signs, his "tells" and knew he was being sincere.

'Good, well before we begin, I should share with you that whilst you desire the pain of submission, I desire the sting of humiliation.'

Christine waved her hand to include the two women sitting opposite her on the sofa.

'These are two of my friends. They are here to add that humiliation. There will be more women, six, at least. They will be introduced slowly, over the coming months, partly to ease you in gently, but mainly because I desire to saviour the experiences to their fullest. So you have a choice, you can walk out and nothing more will be said about a power exchange or you can come in and take off your clothes. My girlfriends are dying to see this cock of yours I've told them so much about. I can assure you, this is what I desire.'

Graham didn't hesitate and entered the living room fully. Whilst he desired the pain another desire warred within him, the desire to serve. It was one he bulked at, one he hadn't, couldn't fully embraced. He was a captain of industry, a man of wealth, power, position and prestige. The images of him kneeling before his wife felt good, felt right, but he struggled with it. Now, here he was standing before his wife *and* other two women. Women he had only ever had a nodding acquaintance with, about to undress and show them his cock, a cock that was raging hard and demanding release from the tight confines of his pants and boxers.

'Well?'

Graham shook off his thoughts and undid the buttons of his shirt. Within a minute he was pushing down his pants and boxers, marching on the spot to work them down his legs and off his feet.

'Men, they have no idea how to undress,' said one of the women.

Pauline, Graham thought. *And the other is... is..... Belinda.*

'Hands on your head,' said Christine.

Graham obeyed.

'Now, as I was saying, pain will be delivered as you desire but gradually, so I can be sure you can take what I give you. I am not so much worried about the hairbrush, paddle or cane across your ass, I think you can take quite a bit there. No, more the pain I intend to inflict on your balls.'

Graham blinked.

'You were right, Christine, he wasn't expecting that,' said Pauline, laughing.

'I told you. So many submissives say they want to submit to the desires of their Master or Mistress but really they want to submit to the fantasies *they* have in their heads, their Master or Mistress merely there to play a role.'

Christine nodded.

'If that came as a surprise, my dear, then you should also know I intend to fuck your ass. Well, I say I. I should say we, me and my girlfriends. All of them, and believe me, you will get all the pain you can handle with the dildos we have chosen. Over the coming weeks you will be fucked by average sized dildos, similar in size to what we girls have to contend with, then something a little bigger, more like that beast you're sporting right there, but after that, dildos with names like, King Kong, The Minotaur, The Anal Destroyer and The Fist will give you some idea of what to expect.'

'Christine fucked me vaginally with the smallest of those named ones and I can tell you I couldn't walk straight for a week,' said Belinda. 'If she came near my ass with that I would have run screaming from the room. The thought of those others....' Belinda shuddered theatrically.

'That's why I will tie you down,' said Christine, looking at Belinda.

Graham smiled at the shocked look Belinda gave Christine but also noted the blush upon her cheeks and knew instantly she had submissive tendencies too.

'You desire pain, and as I say, I will give you that, but perhaps not as you desire, not only at least.'

Graham looked at Christine, waiting, dread and desire warring within.

The both knew where she was heading and one savoured the coming declaration the other both feared and wanted it.

'I'm talking of course about your balls,' said Christine. 'They will provide a great source of amusement for me and a great deal of pain for you. And I will get all the humiliation from you I desire,' Christine added ominously, 'starting now.'

Graham looked at Christine, one eyebrow arched.

'I told the girls what a heavy cummer you are, and they would like to see.'

Whilst he heard the words, Graham couldn't fathom what Christine wanted him to do.

Christine wasn't cross. She hadn't expected instant obedience, instant wavelength connections. In truth that would have spoiled it somewhat for her. She was looking forward to his training, to moulding him to be the submissive she desired. Unlike Graham, she had no inner turmoil of her husband kneeling before her, obeying her, serving her. She was also confident that by the end of the next six to eight months, Graham would not only accept her rules within the power exchange but also the ones she intended to set him for outside too. She would truly become the Head of House, ruling with an iron fist when necessary and giving Graham a short leash within which to live and serve.

Her pussy tightened, tingled and seeped moisture as she squeezed her legs together, enjoying the frisson her thoughts created.

'I want you to knock one out, dear,' she explained, delighting in the instant deepening of embarrassment upon his face, his rosy cheeks from being naked in front of two of her girlfriends now a deeper red and one that covered his entire face.

'I see you are beginning to understand the bargain,' she said.

Graham nodded, turning over the trade off, balancing the books.

'Know that I will never ask you to do something that I do not desire you to do,' said Christine. 'I won't humiliate or degrade you for the sake of it.

Everything I ask of you will arouse and please me. So I guess, the question is, do you wish to arouse and please me?'

Graham nodded and without conscious thought, his fingers curled around the shaft of his cock, his hand moving before his consciousness became aware of his actions.

As his hand moved he looked, first at his wife, the shining excitement within her eyes, the blush of arousal upon her chest evidence of her desire and pleasure, looks mirrored by Pauline and Belinda. Confidence surged within him and his hand moved with familiar ease. Humiliation still burned within him, that hadn't diminished, but the knowledge he was pleasing his wife, his mistress balanced his mind, allowing him to fully give himself to the task.

As the cum boiled within his sack he bit his bottom lip and looked at Christine, unsure whether he was just supposed to ejaculate, spurting his cum into the air and over everything and doing something else.

Christine held his gaze, a small smile playing on her lips as she intuitively knew of his dilemma.

Graham's hand didn't falter, his orgasm soaring as his arousal was fanned by his wife's display of control and power over him. Sweat broke out upon his forehand as he fought against the urge to give his body the reins and ride the climatic wave that was building within his balls and cock.

Christine waited for as long as she dared. Walking a fine line between maximising her exercise of control, for the enjoyment and benefit of them both, and having him shoot all over her lounge, Christine savoured the deliciousness of the scene for as long as she dared.

'Pauline,' Christine snapped.

From the shocked look on Pauline's face, as first she looked to Belinda, then to Christine as if she had not heard correctly, she clearly hadn't been expecting the command but with just that moment's hesitation she was down on her knees, taking his enormous head into her mouth, her tongue swirling over the crown, her cheeks hollowing as she sucked.

'Just a few more seconds,' said Christine. 'You can hold it for that long can't you, for me?'

Graham nodded, his concentration fully focused on holding back the tsunami of an orgasm.

'Now.'

Graham groaned, his hand powering up and down hard before it stopped suddenly.

Christine knew that was the moment the first spurt had erupted. She didn't need Pauline's bulging eyes to confirm it either. Well experienced herself, she knew Graham would pump out four full spurts of cum, and then would need further pumping to draw up more from the reservoir waiting to be released. Orgasms rippled through her as she imagined it, drawing on her own memories, Pauline's mouth being flooded with hot salty cum, so thick it would ooze down her throat. Before one mouthful had even cleared, another would shoot into her mouth, the third joining what was left of the second, and the fourth adding even more to that. Add Pauline being a lesbian, and it just sent her arousal through the roof and Christine's body tingled and pussy tightened as orgasms rippled through her.

'You had better not spill a single drop,' warned Christine, practically hugging herself. She couldn't believe it, this was better than she had imagined it, better than she had fantasised it, ever since Graham had first hinted of a intimate power shift.

Graham couldn't see but also knew Pauline's mouth and throat would be working overtime to get it all down before more followed. All this happened in mere moments. He looked at Christine who smiled warmly and nodded, before firming his grip once more and pumping hard, drawing up the reserves, flooding her with a fifth, sixth, seventh, eighth spurt. Although less, they still amounted to a prodigious volume.

'Keep sucking,' Christine command.

Graham squealed and wriggled, Pauline having to hold onto his hips to stay connected, to obey her Mistress's command, sucking hard at his quickly softening cock.

'Stand still and take it,' Christine commanded.

Graham instantly froze; only his head shaking, high pitched whining sounds coming from his mouth as Pauline took her revenge, not only sucking but wanking his cock with her hand, ensuring the bulbous head got nearly all the attention as she found that's when he squealed the loudest.

After a good couple of minutes, Christine relented, more because the effect on Graham seemed to be lessening, the sensitivity desensitising, then any mercy.

'Good,' said Christine. 'Before, Pauline, Belinda and I spank your ass until it's beetroot red, Pauline, you hesitated before obeying my command. Strip!'

Graham watched as Pauling immediately leapt to her feet, fingers already undoing buttons, and was impressed with her alacrity.

'I will expect nothing less from you, my dear,' said Christine, looking at Graham, one again demonstrating her ability to read his thoughts.

Graham nodded, his cock twitching as Pauline pushed down her panties to stand naked, hands on head.

'Naughty boy,' said Christine. 'This is not for you. Face the wall, hands on your head.'

Graham obeyed, disappointment clear upon his face causing Christine to chuckle.

'I can see this is going to be so much fun.'

Graham's heart bloomed with warmth and his spirits soared as he faced the wall, his cock slowly hardened as the sounds of a spanking, together with Pauline's cries slowly growing in volume, filled the room. He knew his turn was coming, and he felt both anticipation and trepidation at the thought.

The Submission of Graham
CHAPTER TWO
A TEACHING OPPORTUNITY

Graham gasped and held his breath as Christine ran her fingers over his cock.

'I won't harm you,' she said.

'I know.'

'But I want to hurt you.'

'I want that too.'

'Upstairs. I think I need to gag you.'

Christine smiled as she felt his cock twitch.

'Denise?'

Denise looked at Graham and then at Christine before nodding.

Christine's smiled widened.

'Come.'

With her hand firmly on Graham's cock, she led the way upstairs and into their bedroom, complete with several new pieces of furniture.

'Let's stand him in place whilst we gather our toys,' she said, tugging hard on his cock to get him moving once again.

'Ginger or chilli?' asked Denise, holding up two containers full of lubricant.

'Chilli of course,' said Christine. 'No pain will be spared today.'

Denise's anticipatory grin was so delightful Christine laughed and Graham groaned.

'I do believe your wicked side is slowly emerging,' said Christine.

Denise blushed.

'Is it awful?'

Graham shook his head.

'Hot as hell.'

With a grin of pleasure and gratitude, Denise placed the ginger container down and brought the chilli one closer, placing it on the dresser before pressing the top, collecting a generous amount within her hand.

'Oooohhh, I can feel it getting warm in my hand,' she cooed.

'I gave Caroline some,' said Christine, her pussy tightening in pleasure at the look of consternation that flashed across Christine's face. 'She won't use it until we are all together mind. That was one of my conditions.'

'One?'

'The other was that she uses it on your ass first.'

'My ass? Of course, where.......'

Denise gasped and covered her crouch with one hand, just remembering in time, her other was full of liquid gel.

'It's so hot in my hand,' she said. 'In my pussy....'

'You face,' said Christine. 'Caroline will be so vexed with you for missing it. Your eyes are so wide right now, it's.......... orgasmic.'

Christine enjoyed the ripples of pleasure that tingled through her.

'Your ass will burn and sting with this one,' said Christine, picking up the container. 'But your pussy....... it will be so much more. Come, to matters at hand. Coat the dildo atop the standing pole and let's get Graham settled upon it.'

Denise shook off the images and thoughts that were whirling around her mind, hardening her nipples, tightening her pussy and threatening to tip the orgasm that was building nicely over the edge.

It would seem I have inherited Dad's enjoyment of pain, she mused as she coated the phallus atop the pole with a liberal about of gel. *Odd given we aren't actually related*, her mind added. *Something to ponder within my thesis.*

'Done,' she said aloud.

Christine knelt and lowered the pole a little.

'On you pop,' she said.

Graham stood on the wide wooden base, straddling the pole, grunting as Christine pushed the dildo up between his cheeks and into his rectum without pause or delay.

'Hush up,' she said, slapping his ass with a smarting smack. 'A bit higher just for that.'

Pushing the pole upwards forced Graham onto tip toes, the dildo stretching his anal ring and filling his ass, the lubricant warming the sensitive lining.

'Watch how his cock hardens as the chilli gets to work,' said Christine, stepping back, viewing her handy work with satisfaction.

Denise nodded, her eyes darting to Graham's cock as she pulled out the box full of sex toys.

Graham gasped.

'Use the penis gag,' said Christine. 'He hates the connotations it has.'

Denise laughed.

'You really are wicked,' she said.

Christine paused; one leg still within her pants the other out.

'He wouldn't have it any other way,' she said. 'Am I right, darling?'

Graham nodded.

Christine stepped out of her pants and, clad only in her bra and panties, walked over to Graham, lifting his head by placing a finger under his chin.

'Let me hear your mantra, sweetie. I don't think Denise has heard it yet.'

'I am your slave. You are my Mistress. Your pleasures are my pleasure. Your desires are my desires. No pain is too great, no humiliation too raw.'

'Very good, my dear,' said Christine. 'I have a little more to add.'

Graham's face burned with humiliation as his eyes caught Denise's wide eyed stared over his mantra, yet he nodded, needing to hear it, needing to add to his life's meaning.

'No degradation too dehumanising.'

Graham blinked before repeating,

'No degradation too dehumanising.'

'Good boy.'

Christine turned away, seemingly dismissing him, sending a wave of submissiveness through him.

I live to serve you, my wife, my Mistress, with all my heart, my body and my soul.

He couldn't see the wink Christine gave Denise but his heart leapt as she turned, gathered him in her arms and embraced him.

'I live to be served by you, my love, my slave, with all my heart, my body and my soul.'

'Awwwww, that's so lovely,' said Denise, dabbing her fingers beneath her eyes. 'Vampire gloves?'

'Oh for sure,' said Christine, 'and I see no reason why you alone should suffer the burning heat within your sex.'

'Already ahead of you there,' said Denise. 'I thought that the moment the idea had sunk into my brain.'

Denise held up several very long cotton buds.

Christine chuckled.

'You are a wicked girl.'

'A chip off the old block.'

'I wasn't aware we had any so thick.'

'I got them off Alice,' said Denise. 'She had the medical rep make up a batch especially for her.'

'How clever of her,' said Christine, taking one of the swabs and running its length between her finger tips, marvelling as the end pushed her fingers apart. 'We'll use two, one with chilli, but first, one without. Let our slave anticipate the additional pain to come. Look, see.'

Denise followed Christine's nod to see Graham's cock standing ridged, so hard it bobbed, unaided, up and down.

'The stand helps,' said Christine, 'but I have no doubt we would have achieved that without the phallus probing his ass right now.'

'It is impressive,' said Denise. 'Especially considering how many times he's ejaculated today already.'

Christine nodded.

'Actually, I had thought of waiting, letting him recharge, but then the agony of dry cumming appealed to me.'

'Dry cumming?'

'Sure. He will orgasm, just like normal, but nothing, or at least very little, will come out. It'll be like a ruined orgasm, in a way, as it removes the pleasure men receive from having their sperm travel and shoot out.'

'Add that to the soreness of his cock and it's going to be a dry arid spell for our slave,' said Denise.

'Not to mention painful,' said Christine. 'And degrading.'

'Degrading?'

'Yes, an area I desire to lead Graham down into. I am also curious whether you will display both the enjoyment of dominance and submission in this area as you have shown in all others.'

'You have mentioned it to Caroline,' said Denise. It wasn't a question.

'I have.'

'You do remember you are her submissive as well, right?'

Denise clapped her hands in glee.

'You hadn't thought of that had you? I can tell, it's written all over your face.'

Christine's mind was turning over this new information, recalling the delicious fun she had had with Caroline as they conjured up torments and trials for their submissives, each seeking to outdo the other in their wickedness and perversity.

'Hey, never mind that now,' said Denise, taking Christine's hand and pulling her out of her thoughts. 'Let's play.'

'Yes, you're right. This is not the time to dwell on such matters,' said Christine. 'Time to begin Graham's descent.'

Denise watched, intrigued as Christine slipped off her panties and walked into the large en-suite bathroom, leaving the door wide open so she and Graham could watch her as she squatted down. She looked up at Denise and then Graham, her embarrassment clear, her cheeks red, though her determination was undiminished as she dropped her gaze and consciously relaxed.

The force her stream issued and the sound of the pee hitting the tiled floor was alarmingly greater than Christine had imagined and heat washed through her from head to toe. She willed it, with all her mind, to end, but her body had a mind of its own and clearly it had decided to empty every fluid ounce of water from her entire body. So much so, Christine practical mind focused on the ever expanding pool of pee with grave concerns for her bedroom carpet at it crawled ever closer.

Denise was on the same wave length as she leapt to Graham, kneeling to drop the pole, pulling the thick dildo from his ass in one quick jerk, causing him to gasp.

'No time, stop that pee from reaching the carpet!'

Graham, being more practically than perversely minded grabbed a towel, only for it to be whisked from his hand.

'Get on your knees, slave and lick it up.'

Denise's orgasm slipped over, just a little from the look of devotion, humiliation and... *joy?*, something to ponder later, that crossed Graham's face, the ripples of pleasure curling her toes and fingers as they cascading throughout her body unstopping as she watched Graham lapping at the ever expanding pool. As an idea caught hold she looked about for a paddle. Eyes alight with passion and excitement she picked up the punishment paddle, thick and large and brought it down across Graham's bottom.

'Assume the correct position, slave. Present your bottom for your Mistress's beating, whilst you keep your head down in the piss as we desire.'

Graham obeyed, pushing his bottom high whilst his head remained close to the floor, his tongue never ceasing despite the smack of the paddle across his ass.

Christine stood, looking down at Graham, her heart aching with love, affection and desire, the curled upon her lips giving away the cruel streak that wrapped itself around those affections allowing her to explore her dark side. Stepping over him and avoiding the wet parts, Christine left the bathroom, sliding past Denise as she lay down another heavy whack with the paddle.

'Denise.'

With a snap of her fingers she had Denise on her knees as she lifted and placed one foot upon the dresser chair.

'As Graham is occupied and I think a reminder of one's place.'

'Yes, Mistress,' said Denise, her tongue licking the drops of pee that hung from Christine's nether lips.

'Nice idea with the paddle, though one should never use punishment items for pleasure.'

'Yes, Mistress.'

'Here, you take this one and I'll take this.'

Denise took the offered paddle and stood opposite Christine, Graham in between, ass high, tongue still lapping the generous pool his Mistress had left him.

The Transformation of Mark
CHAPTER ONE
GRAHAM'S

The club was full, filled with people, women mostly, though the men were well represented. The music, heavy with bass, pulsated and throbbed, its vibrations felt as much as the music heard, not that anyone was listening. The music was merely an accompaniment to the sounds of the whacks, thwacks, cracks and smacks, cries, moans and groans as the clientele enjoyed everything the club had to offer.

Much was the same as when the club had its first special opening months ago, and much had changed.

'What can I say, I like breasts,' said Kelly.

Christine looked at Mark appraisingly and liked what she saw.

'Is he gay?'

'Nope, as straight as they come,' said Kelly. 'Though I cannot speak of the two men with him.'

Christine let out a soft sigh as her pussy gripped tightly.

'He seems happy enough,' said Alice.

'He knows I enjoy his defilement. Mouth more than ass, actually.'

'Good thing they're taking care of each end then,' laughed Pauline.

'I was referring to the physical changes,' said Christine. 'And the clothes. Does he wear any men's' clothes now?'

'No. His work believes he's transgender and treat him almost reverently. They are so scared to be perceived as homophobic they're bending over backwards. My sister and her girls love it as much as I, so that's another string to our bow.'

'Sister?'

'Yes, haven't I mentioned her before?'

Christine shook her head.

'When do I get to meet them?'

'I'll arrange it. Graham too?'

'Of course, you know I like introducing Graham to new people.'

Kelly chuckled.

'I can't believe Mark walks better in six-inch heels than I,' said Alice.

'That's because your Mom didn't hold a cane when you practiced.'

Alice laughed.

'That's true.'

'For a straight guy, his cock's hard enough,' said Pauline.

'Because he knows I'm watching,' said Kelly. 'If I got up and left, he would instantly push those two off him.'

'The one in front is pulling out,' said Alice.

'Watch,' said Kelly.

The man fisted his cock, millimetres from Mark's lips, his cum spurted thickly, clearly visible to the female audience as it shot into Mark's mouth.

'Watch his throat,' purred Kelly.

Clearly, Mark was swallowing the cum as quickly as he could. Replete, the man staggered backwards and sat down. Mark turned his head and looked directly at Kelly, who gave a small cry, her hips humping her hand which was buried between her thighs, fingers deep within her pussy.

Mark smiled, and then grimaced as the man behind buried himself balls deep, his cum shooting into the darkness of his ass.

Kelly cried out again, the slick sound of her fingers within her wet hot passage clear to Christine and Pauline who sat either side of her, despite the music and accompanying sounds.

Pushing himself to his feet, Mark walked over, kneeling before Kelly, taking each of her fingers into his mouth to suck them clean.

'Mistress.'

'Husband, you have delighted me as always.'

'Thank you, Mistress.'

'May I?' asked Christine.

'Of course,' said Kelly.

Christine beckoned Mark to her and gently cupped his breasts.

'They feel so real,' she said. 'And these nipples, they're actually getting hard as I play with them.'

'Alice and Caroline do amazing work.'

'Alice did these?'

'Yes, they're running a little side line business,' said Kelly with a laugh. 'Expensive, though they assured me I got the family and friends rates. I can't whip them or beat them yet, still too new, nor can I clamp the nipples, so I enjoy myself rubbing in Tiger Balm or Chilli Juice, nice and stingy hot. Can't wait to get his cock done.'

'His cock?'

'Yes, I'm having it changed into a vagina.'

'Seriously,' said Christine, exchanging looks with Pauline.

'Yes, and you can call an intervention if you wish, but save your breath and just ask him.'

'Well?'

'If Kelly desires it, I am happy with it,' said Mark.

'So you're a woman trapped in a man's body?' asked Pauline.

'No, I am a man, but my Mistress wishes me to have a woman's body.'

'And you're ok with that, honestly? You can say.'

'I cannot wait,' said Mark. 'Honestly. My Mistress will be pleased and take delight in my new body. That makes me happy.'

'Ummmmm, I need to think on this,' said Christine.

'I need a drink,' said Kelly.

'Yes, Mistress.'

Christine watched as Mark walked across the club, head held high, conscious, no doubt, of the stares his body drew, female breasts, male cock, clad only in suspenders, stockings and heels.

'I think I will take a wander,' said Christine, clearly troubled.

As she wandered around the club she owned, she took in its patrons and, as always, was surprised at the number of submissive men that were present. All the stocks were full, bottoms reddened by hand, belt, paddle and cane. All six Queening chairs were occupied, the spaces beneath each held a man, all but one, that one held a submissive woman. Although in the minority, at "Graham's," submissive women were more than welcome, and they were well represented amongst the various demonstrations of submission and service.

They even numbered amongst her own staff. Dressed in the pale blue uniform of russet skirt, so short everything beneath was on display, tops so tight they moulded to their breasts, nipples hard against the thin fabric.

Few, if any, men got to sample their charms though and not through any restriction but simply because the Dominants' desires were more male centric.

Christine smiled to see several women queuing for the Queens Circle despite there being a rather plush Ladies Bathroom available down the hallway. Her eyes were drawn to one male as he opened his mouth, the stream from above arriving mere moments later. She searched her memory for his name, Sebastian, that was it. The Mistress who sat above him was not his, but one of many that had peed over him since being tied into place. She knew from previous evenings, his reward would be an hour at the glory hole, pleasuring other submissive men so rewarded or punished by their Mistresses. Bi curious at best, Vincent delighted in the knowledge his Mistress was the architect of his denigration, the more debase, the more humiliating it was, the more he cherished his Mistress and the time she had clearly spent thinking of him and the many ways he could please her.

Moving on, she wandered to the punishment/torture area, complete with its Crosses, Benches, Suspensions and the like. All occupied as Mistresses and their invited guests spanked, paddled and caned their submissives' asses.

A new addition to this area was the milking station. After installing the rule of testing for all members, she had sought ideas to further humiliate the male submissive clientele and came up with the Milking Station. Males were bent over a padded top, their cocks pushed through holes beneath where clear plastic tubes were waiting. Suction pulled these cocks until painfully erect and their prostates were stimulated, mostly by their Mistresses. Two fingers were popularly uncomfortable, three fingers punishing for most, especially as their Mistresses sought only the end product, not the pleasures their ministrations might give their slaves. Other stalls within the station allowed the subs to masturbate openly, eager spectators watching intently, the time taken to ejaculate and the volume often gambled upon. Mistresses betting cane strokes upon their slave's backsides, sometimes their cocks, the winner getting to administer them all. The cum produced was captured and could be purchased for the consumption of their male or female slaves, or for some Dominant women who had a liking for the taste.

One glaring omission from the patrons of Graham's Club was Dominant Men. They were not allowed. This was solely a Female Dominant club.

Recognising a cry, Christine was drawn to one of the crosses, spying Steve bound as he jerked and writhed, Caroline watching with evident pleasure as she slowly turned the thick swab sticking out the end of Steve's cock.

'Chilli?' she asked conversationally.

'Surgical alcohol.'

'Is that hollow?'

'It is. I'm planning on filling his bladder with it. It'll burn like buggery every time he pees.'

'Won't it burn whilst inside too?'

'I hope so,' said Caroline. 'That's the plan.'

'Dangerous?'

'I wouldn't have thought so. We made sure the batch was PH neutral so it should just sting. A lot.'

'Alice on hand?'

'She's aware of the timing so should be along any minute.'

Christine nodded.

She was a little sceptical of the experimenting Caroline and Alice did in pain delivery, but so far no one had suffered any lasting effects or required any medical attention, so she had to concede they knew what they were doing.

Christine waited until the tube was attached to the end of the swab and the alcohol flowed, experiencing several orgasms as Steve's body went into spasm, shaking, jerking and writhing as the stinging liquid stung fiercely all along the length of his cock, and at its base as his bladder began to fill.

'Holes along the swab allow Steve to gain a...... prequel of what's coming,' said Alice.

Christine nodded.

'If this is successful, I think Graham will spend some time up there, I'm so tight and wet it's delicious.'

'I am confident the pain will be exquisite and lengthy,' said Alice.

'I'll return in due course,' said Christine. 'I wish to find Graham.'

'Find Cassie, you'll find Graham.'

'Don't I know it. I'm afraid that girl will get hurt one of these days but nothing I say will dissuade her of her feelings for him.'

'They are genuine,' said Alice.

'I agree,' said Caroline. 'Give the girl the benefit of the doubt and assume she knows he will never leave you for her and allow her the access you freely give.'

Christine nodded. She had tried, as gently as possible, to encourage Cassie to follow in her sister's footsteps and get herself a boyfriend. Paul was so enamoured with Heidi, everything she had asked of him he had willingly given and would no doubt be around the club somewhere, naked except for his collar and leash, kneeling by Heidi's side. But to no avail. Cassie was infatuated or perhaps truly in love with Graham. She certainly loved being his Mistress and, so far, remained inside the boundaries Christine had set for all the women who enjoyed Graham's submission.

The relationship with Cassie's entire family had gone from strength to strength. Vincent's confidence in his dominance over his family had grown, and invitations flowed between the two households frequently. Social evenings which nearly always included Judith and sometimes the girls getting spanked. Graham often being invited to turn one or other over his knee to administer a spanking himself, something he admitted to Christine, he enjoyed thoroughly. He also had shared that Vincent was constantly encouraging him to assume the dominant role within his own family, hinting at weekends of spankings for all the girls merely awaited his elevation to Head of his Household. Graham, though sexually aroused by such an idea, knew enough not to voice such feelings, though Christine's arched eyebrow whenever the conversation included male dominance of any nature or duration was enough to suggest she was reading his mind.

Judith admitted, whilst she loved Vincent's dominance, it was humiliating to be spanked in front of anyone, especially Christine, knowing her beliefs in Female Dominance and the girls shared their embarrassment was heightened by Graham's presence, not to mention when he took them over his own knee, which was mortifying, given their dominant position over him.

Christine loved it all, enjoying the tingles and pussy tightening visuals as well as the full knowledge of the girls' thoughts and feelings, not to mention their eagerness the following day or so to redress the balance with Graham, submitting him to multiple spankings and other humiliating acts of submission as she sat royally surveying it all. Her latest enjoyment was taking Denise around to see Vincent, asking him to take any measures he saw fit to discipline her daughter as her husband was at work, delighting in conjuring up all manner of misdemeanours to encourage Vincent's imagination. Spankings were always on the cards, but with Christine's encouragement, additional punishments were becoming the norm too. Mouth washing for Denise's argumentative ways, and pussy spanking for her wanton behaviour were two, with Christine working to include more sexual orientated punishments that she hoped would transfer to Judith's punishments to be witnessed during their social visits. Masturbation being the first, Denise, suffering the punishment for embarrassing her mother whilst out shopping, had, twice so far, had the indignity of masturbating herself to orgasm whilst Vincent watched, wide eyed and hard. Christine knew it was only a matter of time Vincent would order Judith to do the same whilst she and Graham watched. Of course, she could simply order Judith to do this herself, but there was something to be said for the unknown, not knowing just what punishments Vincent had in store for Judith from one visit to the next.

She spied Cassie, head thrown back, clearly in the throes of climax, and, as she approached, saw Graham, upon his knees, head between Cassie's thighs worshiping her pussy. Heidi sat alongside, head similarly thrown back as Paul lavished his worship in similar fashion. The pair had drawn quite a crowd of onlookers so Christine guessed they had been enjoying the men's attentions for some time.

Stepping next to Cassie, Christine stroked her hair gently, until she opened her eyes and smiled.

'Enjoying yourself?'

Cassie nodded.

'I think it's time I got something out of this, don't you?'

Cassie wet her lips before she nodded.

'Remember, you don't have to enjoy it, or like it even, just show your obedience and accept it.'

'I know,' said Cassie. 'And I accept.'

'That's my girl.'

'We're still coming over tomorrow though, right?'

'Of course. Remember, if you want to torture his balls, don't let him cum tonight.'

'Oh don't worry, he won't be,' said Cassie.

Christine's attention was drawn to Heidi.

'Everything ok?'

'Paul gets jealous when I play with Graham.'

Christine nodded.

'As he should.'

Kneeling, Christine took Paul's chin in her hand.

'You job is to obey your Mistress, pleasure her, please her. If her pleasure includes other men, and or other women, that's for her to enjoy and you to suffer without complaint. Understood?'

Paul nodded.

'Good boy. Heidi, bring him over to the spanking horse and we'll punish him together.'

'Can I come?' asked Cassie.

'Of course,' said Heidi. 'You know I am happy to share him with you.'

Cassie smiled warmly.

'When I get a boyfriend, I'll share him with you too.'

'I know, Sis.'

Cassie and Heidi hugged.

'Come, slave.'

Heidi tugged the leash and Paul obediently crawled along behind the three women.

'He's well trained,' said Christine.

'In most things,' said Heidi. 'His jealousy and attention seeking can be a bit cloying.'

'That's why we are going to punish him,' said Christine.

'Milking station?' asked Cassie, her eyes alight with excitement.

'Good idea,' said Heidi. 'He finds that so humiliating.'

The Humiliation of Paul
CHAPTER ONE
FIRST DAY

'Christina, are you paying attention?'

'Errr, yes?'

'So you can tell me one of the Tragedies Shakespeare wrote?'

'Errrm, Midsummer Night's Dream?'

'That's a comedy, Christina, something you would know if you had been paying attention. Front and centre.'

Paul looked from Christina to Miss Sheppard, wondering what was about to occur, his cock stirring beneath his skirt. He slipped his hand beneath, pulling at the navy panties, so clearly not designed for the male anatomy.

Knickers, he mentally corrected himself. *In England they call them knickers.*

'Skirt and knickers off, young lady. This is not the first time I have had to reprimand you in this lesson. Just because it's your first day, and your first lesson, doesn't mean you do not have to give me 100% of your attention.'

'But, Miss.'

Paul blushed and dropped his eyes as Christina looked towards him, then back to Miss Sheppard.

'Oh, yes, I see. Paul, would you step outside, please? Christina, hurry up, please.'

Paul walked as slowly as he dared, his head looking straight ahead, his eyes though, straining to look left as Christina undid her skirt just as slowly, her head looking down, her eyes straining to look right to see if he had left yet.

Paul left as Christina let her skirt fall, swearing she would get even with Paul under her breath despite the door closing behind without him seeing anything.

In the hall, Paul waiting nervously. It occurred to him he hadn't been given a hall pass, so his attention was split between searching the hallways, listening for the sounds of footsteps and trying to peek through the glass panel within the door, as he listened to the sounds of the spanking Christina was receiving. The sounds stopped quite quickly, and the lesson resumed, leaving Paul wondering whether he should return or wait to be summoned. The sound of heels approaching made up his mind, and he knocked on the classroom door.

Miss Sheppard looked over, clearly surprised, before waving him in.

'Take your seat, Paul. I'm sorry, I forgot all about you.'

Titters greeted this as Paul made his way to his desk.

'Ok,' said Miss Sheppard, wiping the list of Shakespeare Tragedies and Comedies off the board. 'Let's have some fun. Quick fire round. In order, name a Shakespeare Comedy. Christina, you first.'

'Midsummer Night's Dream,' she said promptly.

One by one, the girls in the class answered, leaving Paul in a panic. He had been out of the class whilst Miss Sheppard discussed the Comedies, so didn't have an answer.

'Paul?'

'Errrr, Romeo and Juliet.'

'Romeo and Juliet? Seriously?' said Miss Sheppard. 'One of the most famous tragedies ever written. Front and centre.'

Whilst one would have expected giggles or comments, the class fell completely silent. The girls holding their breath as Paul slowly stood and made his way to the front.

'Err, Miss Sheppard,' he said.

'Yes?'

Paul indicated the class then himself by brushing down the front of his skirt.

'Yes, I see,' said Miss Sheppard, frowning. 'Quite the conundrum.'

She tapped her chin as she thought, leaving Paul standing in front of the class and the girls looking at each other wide eyed and hopeful.

'Well, there is nothing for it,' said Miss Sheppard. 'I can't send the entire class to wait in the hall.'

The girls breathed out, disappointed, they clearly expecting leniency but hoped for a spanking. Miss Sheppard on the other hand.....

'You'll have to take your spanking in front of the girls and just deal with it, skirt and knickers off.'

Paul's mouth dropped open.

'Quick as you can.'

Paul looked at Miss Sheppard, hoping to see something, a twinkle of mirth perhaps, but grey steely eyes looked back.

'Now.'

With trembling hands, Paul undid the clasp, push down the zip and let the material fall to the floor. The navy knickers soon followed, leaving Paul cupping his cock and balls, blushing profusely.

Miss Sheppard looked him up and down, a smile creasing her lips.

'Turn and face the class, hands on head. We might as well get it over with.'

Unmoving, Paul was frozen to the spot.

'I will send you to see the Head Mistress, your Aunt, if you fail to do as you are told, young man.'

Paul's hand fell to his side instantly, and he spun around.

Gasps, titters and giggles rippled around the classroom.

'Ladies, please,' said Miss Sheppard, checking out Paul's equipment, her eyes widening. 'Paul here is very generously endowed. Eighteen, right?'

'Yes, Ma'am.'

'Still growing then, very nice. Ok, let's get this done, or you'll be late for your next class.'

Over Miss Sheppard's lap, Paul stared at the ground as his bottom reddened, though no matter how hard and how long she spanked, his face was redder by far, though the heat and sting soon occupied his thoughts, his feet kicking, his fists drumming and still Miss Sheppard spanked away.

'Miss,' said Christina, raising her hand. 'MISS!'

Miss Sheppard looked up, blinking as she took in the classroom of girls, before looking down at the rosy red cheeks of Paul over her lap.

'Oh, yes, right,' she said, flustered. 'Stand up, Paul, hands on your head as the girls leave. QUIETLY.'

Paul stood too more gasps and giggles.

'I said QUIETLY.'

The girls quietened, but their stares were undiminished as they filed out of the classroom. Miss Sheppard narrowed her eyes.

'Turn around, Paul..... Oh.......'

Miss Sheppard snatched back her hand before it made contact with the enormous erection Paul was proudly displaying.

'My, that really is something,' she said.

'Miss, my next class,' said Paul.

'Yes, yes, quite. Get dressed...... if you can,' said Miss Sheppard's laughing. 'And come and see me tonight, ten minutes to ten. Don't be late.'

'But, Miss, I have to be in my Dorm Room by ten, otherwise I'll be spanked by the Dorm Prefect and if I'm caught by a Mistress, they'll spank me too.'

'Yes, that's true,' said Miss Sheppard. 'And if you're spanked three times within a single day, you are publically spanked by the Head Mistress during morning assembly. So, I suggest you don't get caught.'

Paul held his cock to his tummy as he fastened his skirt before spinning it around, so the zip was at the back.

Miss Sheppard looked at Paul thoughtfully.

'You know, the other Mistresses and I have been wondering what the Head Mistress was thinking bringing you to an all girls school, dressing you in the girls' uniform, having you use the girls' bathroom, changing rooms and dormitories and so on but I am beginning to suspect it is a little less educational as she claims and a little more....... fetish, shall we say.'

'Yes, Miss.'

'Is she really your Aunt?'

Paul shook his head.

'How did you meet?'

'Website, Miss. She was looking for a boy to dress and treat as her niece, and I was looking for a Mistress.'

'A Mistress? So you are submissive then?'

'Yes, Miss.'

'Which explains the erection. I see, I see.'

Paul waited as Miss Sheppard, once again, was lost in her thoughts.

'Miss?'

'Ummmm, oh, yes, run along Paul, there's a dear. Now I know the truth of it, I suspect your life here will be much more........ interesting.'

'Yes, Miss.'

Paul left the classroom at a run, just making it to his next class moments before Miss Jenkins swept into the room.

'Books open, mouths closed,' she barked. 'I'm in no mood for shenanigans this morning.'

*

Paul opened his books, but his mind was in the past.

'I've been offered the post of Head Mistress at a girls' finishing school,' said Liane, 'and I'm looking for something... someone special to take along with me.'

'Yes, Mistress,' said Paul. 'Your profile said you were looking for a male submissive, one you could humiliate constantly, sexually use and abuse 24/7, no limits, no boundaries. That is me.'

Liane nodded.

'Your hair is pretty long now. By the time school term starts it will be perfect. Just needs some styling.'

'Yes, Mistress.'

'I'm not into sadism per- se,' she said. 'Discipline for sure and I suspect the other girls will put you through many tortures and torments so I cannot speak for them and humiliation as I said, plenty of that. You're what, twenty-five?'

'Yes, Mistress.'

'The girls are all younger, yet you will serve them as fully as the Mistresses who are all older, though some only slightly.'

'Yes, Mistress.'

'We will tell them you're eighteen. You can pass for that easily. Dressed as a girl, you'll use the girls' bathrooms, changing rooms, receive the same punishments, and sleep in the same dormitories. I am sure they will quickly adapt and quickly see the potential I offer them. A boy to play with.'

*

'Mr Jefferies. Mr Jefferies. BOY! Are you listening to me?'

Paul snapped out of his reverie.

'Front and centre.'

The class held their collective breath, hugging themselves in glee as Paul once again made the walk to the front of the class, removing his skirt and knickers before bending over, hands on the desk, as Miss Jenkins brought the slipper down hard six times across his bottom.

'Go back to your seat.'

Paul picked up his skirt and knickers and headed back to his chair, making sure to concentrate for the rest of the lesson. He did get a reward of sorts as Frances and Claire were called to the front for talking, both having to remove their skirts and knickers before bending over as he had done for six of the best. He blushed as he realised just how much he had displayed in the same position, Liane's, his Aunt and Head Mistress for all intense and purposes, insistence he was fully waxed ensuring there was nothing left to the imagination, no opening left unseen.

The girls glared at him as they returned to their desks, holding their clothes as if it were his fault somehow. Trepidation and anticipation coursed through his veins as the time ticked slowly towards lunch.

*

'Get in there,' said Christina, shoving Paul into a girls' bathroom. 'What the fuck are you doing here?'

'My Aunt, she's the Head Mistress.'

Claire and Frances exchanged worried looks.

'Perhaps we'd better leave him alone,' said Claire.

'Not likely,' said Christina. 'Get it out.'

Paul looked at Christina, confused.

'Your cock. Jesus, how thick are you?'

'Pretty thick,' said Claire with a laugh.

Christina and Frances laughed.

Paul dropped his skirt and pushed down his knickers.

'Get it hard,' said Claire.

'Wait, I've never seen one before,' said Frances.

'Me neither,' said Christina.

'I've seen my brothers,' said Claire nonchalantly. 'But not hard, just soft like this. Though not as big.'

Christina placed her hand underneath, lifting it.

'It's heavy,' she said, surprised.

'Let me see,' said Frances.

Christina relinquished her place to Frances, who placed Paul's cock in her hand, weighing it thoughtfully.

'It really is,' she said. 'Oh, it's getting bigger.'

The girls crowded together as they watched Paul's cock swell, lengthening until it stood almost upright, the veins along its length rigid.

'Can I touch it?' Claire whispered.

Paul nodded.

Claire wrapped her hand around the shaft, her fingertips just touching.

'Are they all this big? I don't think I can get one this big in me, it's such a tiny hole.'

'It will fit,' said Christina confidently. 'It expands. I've had three fingers in mine so far.'

'Three!' exclaimed Frances. 'I can barely manage two, and that's a tight fit. Nice though,' she added wistfully.

'Do you wank?' asked Christina.

'Course he does. All boys do,' said Claire. 'I have to knock on our bathroom door at home in case my brother is in there, wanking.'

Paul nodded.

'Go on then,' said Christina. 'I want to see.'

'What if someone comes?' asked Frances. 'We should wait. Take him somewhere private.'

Christina frowned before nodded.

'I guess. Do a bit, quick.'

Paul grasped his cock and ran his fist up and down his length.

The girls covered their mouths, stifling their nervous laughter.

'I can't wait to see him shoot,' said Claire.

'Shoot?'

'Yes, when he cums he shoots this white stuff all over. Sperm, you know, the birds and the bees?'

'I know the mechanics,' said Frances. 'Just never seen it.'

'Me neither,' said Christina. 'You know a lot about this sort of stuff,' Claire.

Claire shrugged.

'Mum tells me stuff,' she said. 'I found this sock in Jake's bedroom once. Honestly, it stood up on its own. Mum said he'd been wanking off inside it, the stiffness coming from him shooting his sperm into it. I looked, and it was all white inside.'

'Boys are odd,' said Frances, wrinkling up her nose.

'But now we have one to play with,' said Christina. 'We can find out all about this stuff first hand.'

'I didn't know boys shaved though,' said Claire. 'Jake is all hairy.'

'My Aunt made me,' said Paul. 'She waxed me.'

'Oooooo, I bet that hurt,' said Christina. 'I did that once, never again.'

'Oh I don't mind it. Stings, but it's kinda nice.'

Christina looked at Frances like she had two heads.

Frances laughed.

'What? I do, what can I say.'

'I use a cream,' said Christina.

'I shave, me. Daily,' said Claire.

'So, will your Aunt have you waxed again, when you need it?' asked Christina.

Paul shrugged.

'I expect so. She did it herself. She enjoyed it.'

Frances and Claire exchanged looks.

'She's not your Aunt,' said Christina shrewdly.

Paul looked alarmed.

'You mustn't tell,' he said. 'She'll be cross with me.'

'What will she do? Spank you?'

Paul nodded.

Christine exchanged looks and smiles with the other girls.

'Well....... we won't tell, but we get to spank you instead.'

'Each of us,' said Frances.

'Naked,' said Claire.

'You want to spank me naked?' asked Paul.

'You, silly. Not us.'

'Oh, course,' said Paul, smiling.

'You have a nice smile,' said Claire.

'Oh please,' said Christina, rolling her eyes. 'So we have a deal? We keep your secret, you let us spank you.'

'Deal,' said Paul.

Christina's tummy rumbled, causing everyone to laugh.

'Come on, let's get something to eat.'

Paul left the girls' bathroom together with the girls, chatting amiably about his old school.

Printed in Great Britain
by Amazon

19893863R00149